JUST PASSING THROUGH

Simon saw the two recoilless rifles that had been brought down from the hill behind the house; they were tripod-mounted M-40A1 106mm guns. There was no way any civilian should be in possession of these weapons.

"They had you zeroed in," a voice said.

There was something familiar about the voice, and Simon turned to see who it was. "John Barrone. What the hell are you doing here?"

"I'm just passing through."

Simon shook his head. "We are seventy-five miles from the nearest town. Nobody just passes through this neck of the woods." He looked pointedly at the two M-40s, then over at the bodies of the fugitives. "I'll be damned," he said. "You killed the men who were manning these guns, didn't you?"

"It seemed like the thing to do. They would've killed you," John replied.

"That still doesn't explain why you are here," Simon said. "As far as I know, you aren't with any government-sponsored agency."

"As far as you know," John said.

"All right, I'll ask again. What are you doing here?"

"I told you, I'm just passing through," John said. At that moment a Humvee, painted a lusterless gray, came driving across the meadow, moving through the crowd of government, state, and county officials. The driver honked, and John started toward it. Simon tried to look inside the Humvee, but the windows were so darkly shaded that it was impossible.

"See you around, Simon," John said as he climbed into the Humvee.

<u>BOOK YOUR PLACE ON OUR WEBSITE</u> <u>AND MAKE THE</u> <u>READING CONNECTION!</u>

We've created a customized website just for our very special readers, where you can get the inside scoop on everything that's going on with Zebra, Pinnacle and Kensington books.

When you come online, you'll have the exciting opportunity to:

- View covers of upcoming books
- Read sample chapters
- Learn about our future publishing schedule (listed by publication month *and author*)
- Find out when your favorite authors will be visiting a city near you
- Search for and order backlist books from our online catalog
- Check out author bios and background information
- Send e-mail to your favorite authors
- Meet the Kensington staff online
- Join us in weekly chats with authors, readers and other guests
- Get writing guidelines
- AND MUCH MORE!

Visit our website at
http://www.kensingtonbooks.com

CODE NAME: COLDFIRE

WILLIAM W. JOHNSTONE

PINNACLE BOOKS
Kensington Publishing Corp.
http://www.kensingtonbooks.com

PINNACLE BOOKS are published by

Kensington Publishing Corp.
850 Third Avenue
New York, NY 10022

All Kensington Titles, Imprints, and Distributed Lines are available at special quantity discounts for bulk purchases for sales promotions, premiums, fund-raising, and educational or institutional use. Special book excerpts or customized printings can also be created to fit specific needs. For details, write or phone the office of the Kensington special sales manager: Kensington Publishing Corp., 850 Third Avenue, New York, NY 10022, attn: Special Sales Department, Phone: 1-800-221-2647.

Pinnacle and the P logo Reg. U.S. Pat. & TM Off.

First Printing: May 2002
10 9 8 7 6 5 4 3 2 1

Printed in the United States of America

PROLOGUE

Iraq, January 15, 1991

So barren was the area into which John Barrone, Lieutenant Colonel Arlington Lee Grant, and Sergeant David Clay had parachuted, that they may as well have been on the backside of the moon. Despite their seeming isolation, mission procedure dictated that they operate as if they were under observation; thus they made certain to use shadows and background to eliminate any silhouettes. They called their progress across the desert floor a walk, but they were moving at a ground-eating lope of better than eight miles per hour.

"You are certain he is there?" Colonel Grant asked John.

"He is there," John replied.

John Barrone was the only non-military member of the team. John, Colonel Grant, and Sergeant Clay were engaged in a covert operation, also known as a black ops, though not entirely because the three men were dressed in black and had their faces covered with camouflage paint in order to absorb any ambient light.

John had been operating inside Iraq for several days, looking for General Adbul Sin-Sargon. Once he found him, he'd slipped back across the border to

U.S. Army "Task Force Ripper" to report on his location. When asked to return with the special operations team, John had agreed. One hour earlier, he, Colonel Grant, and Sergeant Clay had made a night parachute jump from a C-130, and were now moving swiftly through the Iraqi desert.

U.S. intelligence sources believed General Sin-Sargon to be Saddam Hussein's most capable battle tactician. He had been the architect behind the Iraq-Iran war, and was now charged with deploying a defense against the coalition forces. Taking out Sin-Sargon would deny the Iraqi Army his leadership and save hundreds of American lives once the invasion started.

Exactly ninety minutes after the three men touched down, they reached their destination. Utilizing the darkness, they were but shadows within shadows as they eased out onto a rock precipice to look down at Sin-Sargon's encampment three hundred yards away.

John and Colonel Grant were carrying M-16 rifles with four double-sized ammo clips. Sergeant Clay was carrying a Heckler & Koch PSG-1 sniper rifle, with a light-gathering telescopic site. As the three men lay there, observing the camp, Sergeant Clay began unloading his magazine, pushing the 7.62 ammunition out one bullet at a time.

"What are you doing?" John asked.

Clay opened a little cloth bag and dumped out a handful of bullets. "I prefer these over the military issue," he said. "I bought them myself, .308 caliber, 168-gram, hollowpoint, boat-tail, match-quality ammunition."

He reloaded the magazine, then clicked it into place just forward of the trigger assembly.

With his rifle loaded and ready, Sergeant Clay deployed the small bipod, then took up a prone firing position, with his left hand just touching the forestock, and his right hand wrapped around the pistol grip. He put his cheek against the receiver, pressed the padded butt into his shoulder, then looked through the scope.

"I'm ready," Clay said.

"Look for a man carrying a carved cane," John said.

"A cane?"

"Sin-Sargon is never without it."

Inside his tent, General Sin-Sargon took a sip of water, then put his cup down beside him. He was sitting cross-legged on a rug, an AK-47 rifle lying across his lap, his jewel-encrusted, gold-headed cane alongside. The tent was dimly lit by a small battery-powered lamp, and there was a double entrance to the tent so that whenever someone entered or exited, they would pass through a closed space. That way, there would be no chance for the light to escape.

"General, if the Americans attack, there will be many of them and they will be strong," Sin-Sargon's aide-de-camp said. "If President Hussein cannot come to some peace, I fear that many of our brave young soldiers will die."

"Those who do not die by the sword will eventually die by some other means," Sin-Sargon replied. "There are many causes of death, but there is only one death. Therefore, if death is a predetermined must, is it not better to die bravely and for a cause? Our cause is righteous and blessed by Allah."

"I believe that as well," Sargon's aide said. "But we are professional soldiers. Many of our men are shopkeepers and goat herdsmen. They have not chosen the art of war, and it is they who fear what lies ahead."

Sin-Sargon stood up. "Perhaps you are right. I will visit them, and remind them that they are fighting for a righteous cause. Bring my cane." He pointed toward his walking stick. The aide picked the cane up and held it reverently.

"Is it true what they say about this cane, General?" the aide asked. "Is it the cane of the Prophet?"

"Yes, that is true. This was the cane of the Prophet Muhammad himself," Sin-Sargon said proudly. "Of course, such a thing is not written, but it has been passed down through many generations of my family, and all of us who have been blessed to own it know in our hearts that it is a true relic of the Prophet. It was also carried by Muhammad II when he wrested Istanbul from the hands of the infidels. And now, it has fallen upon me to safeguard."

Sin-Sargon and his aide stepped into the small canvas alcove. The first flap was closed before the second flap opened, thus preventing any light from escaping. Then, the two men moved out into the night air.

"Here is your cane, General," He handed the walking stick to Sin-Sargon. "I am honored that you have allowed me to hold it."

"I have a target," Sergeant Clay said.

"Take him out," Colonel Grant ordered.

"Damn," Clay said.

"What is it?"

"Mr. Barrone said shoot the man with the cane. But one man has just handed the cane to another. I don't know which one is which."

"The first man was probably General Sin-Sargon's aide, Lieutenant Kahli," said John. "Don't bother about him."

"Kill them both," Grant ordered.

"Colonel, Sin-Sargon is the one we want," John said. "There's no need to kill just to be killing."

"You heard Sergeant Clay. Both men have handled

the cane. The success of this mission is my call. We must be certain. Kill them both, Sergeant."

"Yes, sir," Clay replied.

The PSG-1 rifle boomed, then recoiled against his shoulder, but the flash-suppressor prevented a big muzzle display.

Lieutenant Kahli heard an angry buzz, then a thump. A puff of dust flew up from General Sin-Sargon's shirt, followed by a spewing fountain of blood.

"Uhnn!" Sin-Sargon gasped, his eyes opening wide in shock.

"General!" Lieutenant Kahli shouted, still not comprehending what had just happened. Puzzled, he looked off in the distance, where he saw a quick wink of light. It was the last thing he ever saw, for even as that strange sight was registering with him, the bullet entered between his eyes, then blew tissue, blood, and bone through a half-dollar-sized hole in the back of his head.

ONE

Glenna Rhodes was relatively new to the *Dallas Morning News*, having been a reporter for just over a month. She longed for the day when one of her stories might make the front page, fantasized that she might even get a story above the fold. The story she was working on now, an overrun in the budget for a sewer project, was probably not the story that would do it for her. However, she was of the opinion that if she did the best she could do on any story, no matter what the story was, she would eventually be noticed by the powers that be.

She had just returned from an interview with one of the sewage-plant engineers, the whistle-blower for the story, and was about to begin work on her article when she saw the envelope. It was a brown envelope with no return address, no postmark, and no stamp, and it was addressed to "Newsroom, *Dallas Morning News*."

"Hey!" Glenna called out to the others. She held up the envelope. "Anyone know anything about this?"

A couple of the other reporters glanced toward her. One shook his head, but the others completely ignored her question. They were either on the phone or busy at their terminals, or they figured that Glenna was too new and too green to warrant a response.

"Well, what am I supposed to do with it?" she asked.

"Why don't you open it?" Marty suggested. Marty was at the desk next to hers.

"Okay, I could do that." Glenna bent the clasp, then opened the flap. Pulling out the single sheet of paper, she began reading.

"What is this?" she asked aloud.

"What is it, Glenna?" Marty asked.

"I'm not sure." Glenna picked up her phone and called the Metro Desk. "Andy, this is Glenna."

"I'm glad you called. I'm working on the budget right now. What do you have on the whistle-blower? Anything we can use?"

"As a matter of fact, I think I do have some pretty good stuff, but that's not why I called. I found an envelope on my desk that's a little disconcerting."

"How can an envelope be disconcerting? You are going to have to be more specific about things, Glenna. You're supposed to be a reporter, remember?"

"All right, it is the paper inside the envelope that's disturbing. You want me to describe it to you?"

Andy laughed. "Nah, just hold it up to the phone and I'll look for myself."

"Very funny. This is serious, Andy."

"All right, tell me about it."

"On the top of the page is a drawing of crossed flags. One flag is the Confederate flag, and the other is a Nazi flag. Beneath the flags there is a line in italics. The line is, *'We must secure the existence of our people, and a future for white children.'* I know that sounds weird, but that's what it says."

"Yeah, I know that line," Andy said. "White supremacist groups use it all the time. Some asshole hero of theirs put it in a racist manifesto a few years ago and now it's their 'Give me liberty or give me death' mantra. Is there anything else besides that?"

"Under that, it says, *'Communiqué from The Shield.'* "

"The Shield?"

"Yes, have you ever heard of them?"

"Can't say as I have."

Glenna cleared her throat and began to read. "We, the Shield, in alliance with all Aryan peoples of America, have chosen Dallas to make our statement in fire and blood. To those who would condemn us for our action, we respond by saying that in war there is no discrimination as to age or sex. A dead Jew is a dead Jew!"

"Damn, that's pretty bellicose, isn't it?" Andy said. "Is there anything specific, like, what they are planning to do?"

"No, that's all it says. What do you think, Andy, should I follow up on this? I mean, the sewer story can keep, but this might really be something."

"Is there a return address? Postmark? Date?"

"No, it's in, as they say, a plain, unmarked brown envelope. I just found it lying on my desk."

"Wait a minute, you mean it was just lying there?"

"Yes. I saw it when I came back from the interview."

Andy sighed. "It may not be anything."

"What do you mean it may not be anything?"

"While we were talking just now, I went on the Internet and called up all known white supremacist groups. I don't see any mention of a group called The Shield."

"Nothing?"

"Nothing. Nada. Zilch. I'm afraid someone in the newsroom is pulling your leg. You know, you're new here, probably looking for that one big story that will get you noticed. Just be lucky it's not a story about alien abduction."

"Are you sure there's nothing to this, Andy? I mean, if this is a joke, it's a pretty sick joke, don't you think?"

"Oh, yes, it's pretty sick, all right," Andy said. "And if I find out who did it, there's going to be hell to pay."

"But what if it's not a joke? What if it's the real thing? Shouldn't we at least inform the police?"

"I'd hate to get the police involved if this is just some sort of sick joke. I'd rather keep such things in house. On the other hand I wouldn't want to just stand by and do nothing if . . ." He let his voice trail off in mid-sentence. "Tell you what. I really don't think there is anything to it, but if it will make you feel any better, why don't you go ahead and fax what you've got over to the police and let them have a look at it. I mean, they are better equipped to deal with this than we are."

"All right, but if it turns out to be something, it's my story, okay?"

Andy chuckled. "You've got it, kid. In the meantime, I'm giving you twelve inches on the whistle-blower."

"Twelve inches? That's all?"

"All right, eighteen if you can make it sing."

"I'll have it singing like Luciano Pavarotti," Glenna quipped.

Hanging up the phone, Glenna punched in the fax number for the Dallas Police Department, then sent the communiqué to them to deal with. After that, she put it out of her mind and started working on the story Andy had assigned her.

At the Dallas Police Department, Glenna's message was received and printed. Almost immediately thereafter, another fax was received, this one a six-page document detailing "Dallas's Greatest Selection of Oversized Fashions at Carmack's Big and Tall Men's Shop." That was followed by the lunch menu from

Porgie's Barbeque, then by another fax from an office-supply store, offering a special on ink cartridges. By the time the flurry of faxes had finished, there was a stack of fifteen pages. Walking by the fax machine a few minutes later, Police Clerk Doris King saw the unsolicited advertising flyers.

"There ought to be a law against sending this stuff over the fax machine," she grumbled. "What if we needed it for something important? It would be all tied up."

Scooping up the flyers, Doris dumped them all into the nearest trash can, then emptied the office coffee grounds over them. Among the discarded and coffee-stained faxes, was the "Communiqué," still unread, that Glenna had sent half an hour earlier.

An open box of crayons made a colorful splash on the side of the white van. The driver of the van turned south off Spring Creek and onto Hillcrest. After proceeding north for one mile, the van pulled into a curved driveway. The driveway passed under the portico of a rather sprawling building. A sign in front of the building read: NORTH DALLAS JEWISH CHILDREN'S CENTER.

The tan Ford that was following the van pulled into the drive as well, then backed out so that it was heading north. It waited at the curb while the van driver left his vehicle, locked the door behind him, then walked casually over to get into the car.

Just inside the center, nearly forty children were waiting in the foyer for the chartered bus that was coming to take them to the zoo. All of the children were wearing bright-orange T-shirts stenciled with the logo NORTH DALLAS JEWISH CHILDREN'S CENTER. The bright orange shirts not only advertised the center, but also had the more important function of pro-

viding the field-trip monitors with an easy way of lo-
cating "their" children from among the many who
would be at the zoo.

Barbara Rosensweig, one of the administrators, happened to be standing by the door when she saw the
van pull into the drive.

"Well, now, that's odd," she said, looking through
the door window.

"What's odd?" asked Julian, the center's mainte-
nance supervisor.

"The driver of that van just stopped under the portico, then left his van and walked off."

"Maybe he's come to take the children to the zoo."

Barbara shook her head. "I wouldn't think so. That
van isn't nearly big enough for all the children. And
why would he just walk away like that?"

"Would you like me to see what I can find out?"

"Would you?" Barbara replied. "I mean, if he has
no business here, he really needs to move that van.
Otherwise, he'll block the drive so that the bus can't
pull through."

"I'll check on it for you."

Marvin Keefer was driving the tan Ford north on
Hillcrest. Jay Shelby, who had just left the van at the
children's center, was riding in the shotgun seat. Jay
looked at his watch.

"How much time?" Keefer asked.

"About thirty seconds."

Keefer turned east onto Arapaho.

Back at the children's center, Julian pressed his face
against the window of the van and looked inside. On
the passenger seat he saw a black box. A digital readout was flashing red in a little window. As Julian looked

at the readout he saw numbers ticking down: seven, six, five. It took him a second to realize that this was a timer of some sort. By the time he formulated the thought that this might be the timer to a bomb fuse, it was too late. Even as he was standing there, the van exploded with a huge fireball.

TWO

Transfiguration Episcopal Church was just across Hillcrest from the children's center. Father Ken Pyron was putting a book back on the shelf of the church library when the windows were blown in by the concussion of the explosion. Pyron was cut with flying glass and pelted with tumbling books. The booming sound was so loud that he thought something had exploded just outside the church. When the dust settled, he rushed to the window to assess the damage. That was when he saw the North Dallas Jewish Children's Center.

What had been a large, modern building just a moment earlier was now nothing more than a pile of twisted steel and broken brick. Mixed in with the brick, steel, and burning timbers were several little orange clumps. It took Father Pyron a moment to discern what the orange clumps were. Then, with a sick feeling in the pit of his stomach, he realized the truth. He was looking at bodies . . . children's bodies.

Both Keefer and Shelby heard the explosion as they were driving east on Arapaho.

"Oops, I forgot to yell timber," Keefer said.

Shelby giggled. "Let's see what they have to say about it," he said as he turned on the radio.

Tim McGraw was singing. That song was followed by a commercial, then three more songs and another commercial. After the commercial there was a weather report.

"What the hell is wrong with these people?" Keefer asked. "Don't they ever give any news?"

They were heading north on the North Dallas Freeway, nearly to Allen, before they heard the first announcement over the radio. It came in the way of a bulletin that interrupted a song in progress.

"Here we go," Keefer said as, in breathless excitement, a reporter began to read.

This just in to our newsroom. There has been an explosion of unknown origin at the North Dallas Jewish Children's Center. At this time we do not know the extent of the damage, nor do we have any word on casualties. We are told, however, that there are many casualties, including several fatalities.

The North Dallas Jewish Children's Center is a preschool and day-care facility located on Hillcrest in North Dallas. Police have blocked off Hillcrest and ask that all citizens avoid the area. An emergency number is being established for families to call for information.

"Well, we did it," Shelby said, turning the radio off.

"Yeah. Wonder how many of those little Jew bastards we killed."

"You know, I sort of wish . . ." Shelby started.

"You wish what?"

"I wish we could have hit something else, maybe a Jewish bank, or some civic club, something with adults. I mean, doesn't it bother you a little to know that we probably killed a bunch of kids?"

"Doesn't bother me a bit. Kid Jews grow up to be adult Jews," Keefer replied. "Besides, hitting someplace like this will get us a hell of a lot more publicity.

You remember Columbine High School, don't you? Hell, they harped on that for a year."

"I guess you're right," Shelby said. "But it makes me a little queasy nevertheless."

"Ahh, don't think about it," Keefer replied. "I'm hungry. What do you say we get some Mexican?"

It was dark when Keefer and Shelby pulled into the front yard of the farmhouse that was the current headquarters for The Shield. Getting out of the car, they stretched away the stiffness of the long drive, then went inside. There were half-a-dozen people in the living room, watching television. Images of the bomb-damaged children's center played across the screen.

As soon as Keefer and Shelby stepped into the living room, those assembled stood and applauded.

"Our action unit is back," Luke Clendenning said. He saluted Keefer and Shelby. "Gentlemen, I congratulate you on your mission."

"Thanks. What's the latest count?" Keefer asked.

"According to all the reports, fifty-two injured, thirty-seven dead," Luke replied.

"Only thirty-seven? Damn, I was hoping we'd done better'n that."

"You men look bushed after your long drive," Emma Clendenning said. "Why don't you sit over there? I baked a couple of apple pies today. I'll bring you a piece, along with some coffee."

"Ah, Emma, you're too good to us," Shelby said.

"What can I say?" Emma replied. "It's the mother in me." She hitched up her gun belt as she headed toward the kitchen.

"You boys get a good night's sleep," Luke said. "Tomorrow we're leaving this place and moving our operation to Oregon."

"Hey, Luke, you think folks will stand up and take notice of The Shield now?" one of the others asked.

Luke, the Supreme Commander of The Shield, walked over to the window to look out into the dark. He stood there for a long moment, just staring through the window. Finally, he turned back to the others.

"When Adolph Hitler attended his first Nazi Party meeting, do you know how many were there?" He answered his own question before anyone else could. "Eight. By coincidence, the same number as there are of us. And from those eight dedicated Aryans grew a movement so powerful that it took on the entire world.

"Like those eight, we represent the Aryan race, and like those eight, we will grow into a powerful movement. Hitler failed because he tried to conquer the world before everyone understood the validity of his message. We will succeed because we are not looking to dominate the world, just protect our Christian and Aryan rights. We want only to fulfill the promise of the Fourteen Words. Let us now say them together."

Clicking his heels together, Luke stuck his right arm out in the Nazi salute. The others stood and extended their arms duplicating Luke's salute. In the kitchen, Emma put down the pie, brushed her hands together, then mimicked her husband in holding out her right arm. Speaking in unison, the little group mouthed the mantra.

"We must secure the existence of our people, and a future for white children."

The Dallas Police Department and the Texas Rangers, as well as the FBI and several other federal agencies, began an immediate investigation of the bombing in Dallas. Their high-profile operation was followed closely by the news media. The chiefs of every agency, the station heads, the field officers in charge, and the public information officials granted frequent interviews and conducted daily press conferences to report their progress.

What neither the official law-enforcement agencies nor anyone in the media knew was that the bombing was also being investigated by John Barrone and the group of men and women who worked with him. Unrestricted by technicalities, John and his team were having considerably more luck in determining who was responsible. The clandestine investigative body which John headed was known as the "Code Name Team."

So secret an organization was the Code Name Team that there were very few people who even knew of its existence. A consortium of billionaires and multimillionaires sponsored their operations, and while most of their backers were American, there were also sponsors from England, France, Germany, and Italy, with perhaps two or three from the Scandinavian countries.

The job of the Code Name Team was to take care of things that managed to fall through the cracks of the more traditional law-enforcement agencies. Terrorists, murderers, drug-dealers, and others of their ilk were often set free because of loopholes in the details and niceties of the law. More often than not, those same people would go right back to committing murder and mayhem. Such people were fair targets for the Code Name Team.

The Code Name Team was without government connection, and because they were an extra-legal—if not illegal—operation, they often found themselves at cross-purposes with the government. On the other hand, there were certain individuals within the government who *did* know about the Code Name Team and their mission. These few "friends in high places," sometimes referred to by the Code Name Team members as FIHP, would, from time to time, turn a blind eye to the Code Name Team operations. And on certain, very rare occasions, the Code Name Team might even get some covert assistance from the government through FIHP.

The FIHP was made up of old friends and former partners of John and the others in the team who had managed to maintain their contacts and friendships from their own earlier associations with the FBI, CIA, ASA, and other such agencies.

Because they had no official status, the Code Name Team often functioned under the guise of a private detective agency, private security firm, or bail-bonding operation. If they obtained evidence without a warrant, or violated the personal privacy of a criminal by eavesdropping on a telephone conversation, or hacked into the computer files and e-mail of known terrorist groups, they did so without apology. The information thus obtained was just as valid, and they were committed to use any investigative tool necessary to put such scumbags out of business.

Using cover organizations, and disregarding the privacy rights of scumbags who had no right to privacy, John and his team began unearthing several leads on the terrorist bombing in Dallas.

They tapped telephone conversations, hacked e-mail files, and used an investigative procedure they called "Deep Intrusion" to locate critical evidence. Another term for Deep Intrusion would be "Breaking and Entering."

John got the first major break when he learned that Lucas and Emma Clendenning had recently made a black-market purchase of two recoilless rifles. Lucas Clendenning had referred to himself in the purchase agreement as "Supreme Commander of The Shield."

John knew that a group calling themselves The

Shield had claimed responsibility for the bombing in Dallas. Now he had a connection.

Getting information from some friendly sources in the government, John also learned that the van that was used in the bombing had been traced to a dealership in Fordyce, Arkansas.

The van dealer had reported it stolen nearly a year earlier, so he was not a direct link. However, research turned up the fact that the Clendennings had once lived in Fordyce, and had been residents at about the same time the van was stolen.

From that point on the investigation went faster. It was a little like finding the loose end on a ball of yarn. Once the end of the string is found, the ball can be unwound rather quickly. One clear fingerprint from a fragment of the van was identified as belonging to Jay Shelby, a prime suspect in the bombing of a Jewish synagogue that had taken place two years earlier. Shelby's alleged accomplice in that incident was Marvin Keefer. Through further Internet incursions and tapped telephone calls, John learned that Keefer and Shelby were members of Clendenning's group, the Shield. He also learned that The Shield, recently in Oklahoma, had relocated to the Blue Mountains of Oregon.

Once he had all the intelligence data gathered, John shared the information with the federal agencies that were involved in the investigation. He took the precaution, however, of only providing that information to those "friends in high places" that he knew he could trust. In that way, the Code Name Team's participation in the investigation was not compromised.

When John learned, shortly thereafter, that a joint task force made up of men and women from every involved agency would be conducting a raid against The Shield, he knew that his information had reached the right ears. He knew also that his job wasn't finished. If the raid was going to be successful, the joint task force would need help from the Code Name Team, whether they wanted it or not, and whether they even knew about it or not. To that end, John put his own task force together.

· Thus it was that on the morning of the raid against The Shield, John Barrone and his Code Name Team were already in the field and in position.

THREE

Sky Meadow, Wheeler County, Oregon

Brilliant bars of sunlight filled with millions of glistening dust motes stabbed down through the trees to push away the early morning shadows. In air redolent with the scent of pine needles, a deer stepped from the edge of the forest, sniffed cautiously, then moved down to the small stream that wound its way through a flower-filled meadow. Just as the deer lowered its head toward the water, there was the pop of static and rush of squelch as a two-way radio's carrier wave was activated. The deer lifted its head in quick fear.

"Unit two-seven, move to your left about fifty meters," a radio voice said.

The radio call snapped through the silent woods and the deer, hearing the unnatural intrusion into its world, bolted, darting back into the woods with its white tail flashing.

"Norton, will you for chrissake turn your radio down?" Simon Mason, the agent in charge of Joint Task Force Clean Sweep, hissed.

"Sorry, Chief," Norton said, turning down the offending device.

* * *

Half a mile away from Simon and his fellow agents, John Barrone and three other members of the Code Name Team—Jennifer Barnes, Mike Rojas, and Chris Farmer—were working their way carefully along a ridgeline. Their camouflaged clothing, and the skill with which they moved, made them nearly invisible, even from just a few feet away.

"Contact," John said, whispering into a small lip microphone.

"Where?" Mike asked.

"Look forty-five degrees to your left, then up to the military crest of the hill."

The military crest, Mike knew without having to be told, was just below the actual top, the highest point of a hill one could occupy without being silhouetted against the skyline.

"See that large rock outcropping?" John said. "There are four of them."

"I see them," Jennifer said. "And there are the recoilless rifles. If they open up with those things they'll cut Mason and his men to pieces."

"Are we going to take them out?" Chris asked.

"Yes, but we can't do anything yet," John said, "If we do, we'll compromise Mason's operation. But once the shooting starts, the recoilless rifles are free targets."

"It's not going to be that easy from here," Mike suggested. "They're a good three hundred yards away, and at an up angle."

"Hey, John, have you considered what would happen if they turn those things on us? At this range, they have the advantage," Chris said.

"If they shoot at you, duck," John replied.

Jennifer chuckled. "Damn, now, there's an idea, Chris. We could duck. Why do you suppose we didn't think of that?"

* * *

Simon, unaware that his men were being ranged and targeted by what were, basically, two pieces of light artillery, raised his binoculars. What he saw was an open meadow, filled with wildflowers of every hue and tint blooming in colorful profusion. In the middle of the two-and-one-half-acre field sat a small cabin, approximately one hundred yards distant from Simon's current position. He would have liked to get closer to the cabin, but he couldn't do so without risking exposure in the open field. Sweeping the perimeter of the meadow with his binoculars, Simon could see another group of men slipping through the woods on the other side of the cabin, getting into position, not only for the final assault, but also to block any escape attempt once they were engaged. Simon's group was "Hammer." He called the other group "Anvil."

Simon Mason's assault force was composed of mixed elements from the FBI, the BATF, and the U.S. Marshals. Although Oregon State and Wheeler County law officers were aware of the operation, they were not tactically involved.

Shadowing the operation from a half mile away was the Code Name Team. The team was tactically involved, but operationally independent of Mason. Not only were they operating independently of Joint Task Force Clean Sweep, Simon didn't even know they were there.

"Hammer, this is Anvil," the voice on the radio said. The Anvil team leader was Agent Muldoon of the BATF.

"Go ahead, Anvil."

"Everyone is in position."

"Stand by," Simon said. He lifted the binoculars for one more look at the cabin.

"What are we waiting for, Chief?" Norton asked. "Looks like about everyone is ready. When do we go?"

"We go when Washington gives us the word," Simon answered.

"Hell, they're back in Washington. What do they know about what's going on out here?"

Simon glared at Norton, then pulled out his satellite phone and punched in a number. His call was answered on the second ring.

"Tactics."

"This is Mason. We have the cabin surrounded."

"You're sure that you have found the headquarters of The Shield?" Tactics asked. "We don't want any foul-ups."

"This is the place."

"Lucas Jay Clendenning?"

"He's in there."

"Anyone else?"

"His wife, and, according to our best estimate, about eight or ten others."

"Well, which is it? Eight or ten?"

Simon sighed disgustedly. "Do you want me to go down there, knock on the door, and ask them?"

"I just wish you could be more specific."

"This is as specific as it gets. Do we have clearance or not?"

"You have clearance to proceed."

"What level?" Simon asked.

"To the extent possible, we would like arrests."

"I'm going to have to tell you, it's not going to be that easy to put these folks under arrest. You're going to have to give me more leeway than that."

There was a momentary pause from the other end.

"You still there?" Simon asked.

"Yes, I'm still here."

"You haven't answered my question. What level?"

"Maximum use of force is authorized," Tactics replied.

"Thanks. I'll get back to you," Simon replied, punching out of the phone call.

"Did we get the go-ahead?" Norton asked.

"Yes," Simon replied.

"Can we use maximum force?"

"We can use maximum force," Simon said. He keyed the radio. "Anvil, get ready. I'm going to call them out."

"And if they don't come out? If they start shooting?" Muldoon asked.

"Maximum force."

"Roger that," Muldoon said, the enthusiastic agreement in his voice clearly obvious.

Simon reached for the handheld megaphone, picked it up, and pointed it toward the cabin.

The inside of the cabin was decorated with Nazi flags, SS symbols, and photographs of Hitler. The walls were plastered with posters proclaiming white power and strident slogans and a stitched, rose-embossed sampler of the Fourteen Words.

The layout of the cabin was basically one large room with cooking facilities on one end, a dining table in the middle, and bunks on the other end of the room. There was a small curtained-off area on the other side of the kitchen to provide some privacy for Lucas and his wife.

Lucas, Keefer, Shelby, and two others were just sitting down to a breakfast of potatoes and eggs being served by Emma. Five assault rifles leaned against the table, while Emma had a pistol strapped around her waist.

"How come you didn't cook any bacon or sausage?" Keefer asked.

"We used up the last of the bacon yesterday. Ran out of sausage three days ago," Emma answered.

"We'll get some more supplies up here in a day or two," Clendenning promised. "You boys hurry up with your breakfast, then go up on the ridge and relieve Cooper and the others on those recoilless rifles."

"You know, I almost hope the Feds do try somethin' while I'm on one of those guns," Keefer said. "I'd like to blow 'em all to hell."

"You just keep your eyes open out there, Marvin," Clendenning ordered. "We don't want anyone sneaking up on us."

"When you hear all hell breaking loose, you'll know I spotted them," Keefer replied.

Outside the cabin, Simon keyed the talk switch on the bullhorn. The moment he did so, there was a loud squawk.

Back inside, everyone heard the squawk.

"What was that sound?" Emma asked, looking toward the window.

"I don't know, but I heard it, too, and I aim to find out," Clendenning replied. Getting up from the table, he grabbed his rifle, then stepped over to the window and looked outside.

"See anything?" Emma asked anxiously.

"Nothin' yet," Clendenning replied, searching the tree line.

"Clendenning, we know you are in there!" an electronically enhanced voice called. "Your cabin is completely surrounded! Come out with your hands up!"

Clendenning picked up a two-way radio. "Cooper! You guys blind up there? The Feds are here!"

"I see one of the bastards now," Eddie Finch said. There was the sound of breaking glass as Eddie crashed the barrel of his rifle through the window in order to get a shot. He fired, and a federal agent grabbed his chest, then tumbled backward. "I got the son of a bitch!" Eddie shouted happily.

"All units, open fire! Open fire!" Simon shouted into his radio.

Right on the heels of Simon's order came the whooshing sound of an incoming round. A shell exploded high in one of the nearby trees, causing pieces of shattered limbs and bark to rain down on Simon and his men.

"Jesus! What the hell was that? Where's it coming from?" Norton yelled, looking around in fear.

From Anvil's position on the other side of the cabin, agents began firing. Simon could see winks of fire and puffs of smoke from behind the trees and rocks. As the bullets slammed into the cabin, more glass shattered and wood splintered.

The firing wasn't all in one direction, for muzzle flashes winked back from the little cabin as well.

Another round exploded over the heads of the task force.

"Jesus! They've got artillery!" Norton shouted. "We've got to get out of here!"

"Hold your ground!" Simon ordered.

Some distance from Simon and the task force, John Barrone and the others from the Code Name Team had maneuvered into position to fire at the recoilless rifles.

"Take 'em out!" John ordered. As one, the Code Name Team fired. Three of the men on the recoilless rifles went down with the first volley. The fourth required an additional shot.

"What?" Mike asked when the others looked accusingly at him. "So I missed the first shot. The sun got in my eyes."

* * *

Inside the cabin, Clendenning and the others were staying as low as possible. The bottom part of the cabin walls had been reinforced with plates of steel, thus providing them with some degree of protection. Even so, the bullets continued to whiz through the cabin, breaking crockery and smashing into the walls on the other side.

"Where's our big guns?" Keefer asked. "How come our boys aren't shootin' anymore?"

"I don't know," Clendenning answered. He looked over toward his wife. Emma was crouching down in fear behind the steel-reinforced cabin walls. "Emma, don't just lie there, goddamnit! Get off your ass and help! There's more ammunition in the chest! Get it, and get it passed out!"

With her eyes pinpoints of fear, Emma nodded, then got up and started across the room toward the chest. Clendenning was looking right at her, and was about to warn her to crouch down a little, when he saw the back of her head explode from the hydrostatic impact of a bullet slamming into brain tissue.

"Emma!" he shouted, going toward her. Kneeling beside her, he saw that she was dead, instantly killed by the bullet that had struck her in the head.

"Bastards!" Clendenning shouted, running back to the window and resuming his firing. "You killed Emma, you ZOG bastards!"

Clendenning saw a federal agent trying to improve his position by darting from a tree to a nearby rock. He fired, and saw the agent go down.

"Hammer, we've got two more men down here," Muldoon called over the radio. "That makes three on this side."

"Three dead?" Simon asked.

"Two are dead. The other is going to be if we don't get him to a hospital soon."

"Mason, Tucker is down!" Norton said.

"Damn," Simon said. "That's four men." Simon looked back toward the ridge. "Can anyone see where those explosive rounds are coming from?"

"They've stopped shooting," Norton said.

"I hope they stay stopped."

"What are we going to do?" Norton asked. "There's too much shooting coming from the cabin to rush it."

"Let's get some tear gas in there," Simon ordered. "Maybe we can flush them out."

"Right," Norton said. He picked up an M-49 grenade launcher, took a canister from a canvas bag, loaded the weapon, then fired it toward the cabin. The canister looked like a football thrown in a perfect spiral as it sped toward the window, marking its trajectory by a trailing stream of smoke. One second after it smashed through the window, the inside of the cabin was lit up with a brilliant flash.

"What the hell?" Simon asked. "I've never seen a tear gas canister do that."

Norton looked into the ammunition bag, then picked up one of the missiles.

"Damn, Chief, that wasn't tear gas, that was an incendiary shell."

Simon saw two more missiles slam into the house from the Anvil positions. These too were incendiary shells, Muldoon obviously taking his cue from the one Simon fired. With three firebombs detonating inside the cabin, the wooden structure quickly caught on fire.

Simon picked up the bullhorn and pointed it toward the house.

"Clendenning! Come out! You and your men come out now with your hands up and we won't fire!"

There was no answer.

"Is your wife with you? If she is, send her out. There's no need for Emma to die with you. I promise, we won't fire at you."

"You've already killed her, you ZOG bastards!" Clendenning shouted.

"Zog?" Norton asked.

"It means Zionist Occupied Government," Simon explained dryly. He raised the bullhorn again. "Come on out, Clendenning! Come out before it's too late."

The front door of the cabin opened.

"Hold your fire, men. Hold your fire," Simon ordered, shouting through the megaphone.

Suddenly four men dashed out. Instead of coming out with their hands up, though, they came out firing. The federal agents returned fire, pouring hundreds of rounds toward the men. Quickly, the four men went down.

"Cease fire!" Simon shouted through the bullhorn. "Cease fire, cease fire!"

Finally, the last bullet was fired and the final echo rolled back from the hills. Now, except for the crackling sound of the burning cabin, all was quiet.

One of the federal agents started toward the four fallen men, but amazingly, one more rifle shot rang from inside the cabin. The agent went down, even as the others began pouring fire into the building. Again, Simon shouted for a cease-fire, finally succeeding in getting the shooting stopped.

Once more the Umatilla National Forest fell silent, except for the snap and roar of flames. By now the building was a blazing inferno, totally involved and pouring smoke from every window.

This time the agents were much more cautious, and it was several minutes before any of them ventured forward.

"What do you think, Chief?" Norton asked.

"You remember the robot character Arnold Schwarzenegger played in that movie?" Simon asked. "*The Terminator?*"

"Yeah, I saw that movie," Norton said. "It was a good picture. 'I'll be bock,' " he said, laughing as he gave his impersonation of Schwarzenegger's famous line.

"Well, if anyone is still alive in there, it would have to be someone like the Terminator," Simon said. "Any humans still in there are crispy critters."

"Mason, this is Muldoon."

Simon keyed the radio mike. "Yeah, Muldoon, go ahead."

"I just sent Abbie and Tom up to check on those recoilless rifles. You know, the ones that were firing at us at the beginning?"

"Yeah, what happened to those guys anyway? They only fired about two rounds, then quit. Did they get away?"

"Get away, hell. They're dead, all four of them. I don't know how you did it, but it was a good job taking them out."

Clicking off the radio, Simon looked over at Norton. "That's strange."

"What?"

"The guys who were raining artillery down on us are dead." He looked around at the others. "Did any of you guys take on a target other than the cabin?"

The other agents looked at each other questioningly, then shook their heads. "No, we were all firing toward the cabin," one of them said.

Simon clicked on the radio. "Muldoon, you sure none of your boys took 'em out?"

"No, we didn't do it. What are you telling me, that you didn't do it either?"

"That's what I'm telling you."

"Then who the hell did it?"

"Could've been one of their own, I guess," Simon

said. "Maybe he panicked, shot his friends, then bugged out."

"Yeah, well, I don't care who did it, long as it was done," Muldoon replied.

"Bring your wounded down," Simon said. "I'm calling in medevac."

Half an hour later the area around the cabin was crowded with people. The federal agents and state and county law-officers were wearing dark blue jackets, with their agencies printed on the back in big, yellow letters. There were also a handful of reporters, taking photographs and conducting interviews. The reporters were all wearing I.D. badges pinned to their breast pockets.

Simon was talking to one of the reporters. As a medevac helicopter lifted off with its load of wounded federal agents, the rotor-wash whipped the heads of the wildflowers into a frenzy. Not yet evacuated were the bodies of eight members of The Shield. They lay in lumps under rubber sheets. The Shield dead included the bodies of the four men that had been dragged down from the hill. From the smell that was permeating the area, everyone could tell that there were more bodies in the smoldering ruins of the burned cabin, but for the time being, it was still too hot to look for them.

The Indian paintbrush, oxeye daisies, and purple lupines that waved peacefully in the sun-splashed meadow belied the carnage that had so recently taken place.

"Agent Mason," the reporter said, raising his voice to be heard over the sound of the departing helicopter. "If you were going to rate this, which government debacle would you most compare it to? Ruby Ridge or Waco?"

Simon glared at the reporter. "You trying to make trouble?"

"No, sir, I'm just trying to get a story, that's all. Looks to me like you had a slaughter up here."

"This was a legitimate operation, consisting of elements from several agencies," Simon answered in exasperation. "I wouldn't compare it to either of those incidents."

"You wouldn't? Well, what would you compare it to? Three of your men were killed and two were wounded. And you killed at least eight of the fugitives, maybe more, depending on what we find in the cabin when it's cool enough to search."

"What happened here couldn't be avoided."

"It's becoming increasingly clear that the official solution to everything is to just start shooting indiscriminately," the reporter said. "We are seeing that everywhere we look now, from city police to highway patrols to the FBI."

"As far as I'm concerned, we owe these men a debt of gratitude," Glenna Rhodes said. Because she had been on the story from the beginning, she was here on special assignment from the *Dallas Morning News*. "I saw the dead children at the center in Dallas. You didn't," she said to the obnoxious reporter.

"One slaughter does not excuse another, Miss Rhodes. These men should have been arrested and brought to trial," the reporter insisted. "Now their guilt will never be proved. Agent Mason here has taken it upon himself to be judge, jury, and executioner."

Simon stared at him for a long moment, making no effort to hide his disgust. "If you'll excuse me, I've got to get back to work," he said, walking away.

Simon saw the two recoilless rifles that had been brought down from the hill behind the house, and he squatted down for a closer examination of them. They were tripod-mounted, M-40A1 106mm guns. There was no way any civilian should be in possession of these weapons, though Simon knew they could be bought from international arms dealers for around twenty thousand dollars each.

"They had you zeroed in," a voice said.

"Yeah, they did," Simon answered. He sighed. "You know, when I came into this business, all we had to worry about was a few Saturday Night Specials. Now we're going up against artillery. What surprise will they have for us in the future?"

"Whatever it is, you'll just have to be ready for them. That is, to the degree the agency will let you. Otherwise, you'll be bringing a knife to a gunfight."

There was something familiar about the voice, and Simon turned to see who it was.

"John Barrone," he said. "What the hell are you doing here?"

"I'm just passing through," John replied.

Simon shook his head. "We are seventy-five miles from the nearest town. Nobody just passes through this neck of the woods." Simon looked pointedly at the two M-40's, then over at the bodies of the fugitives. "I'll be damned," he said. "It was you, wasn't it?"

"What was me?"

"Don't play games with me. You know exactly what I'm talking about. You killed the men who were manning these guns, didn't you?"

"It seemed like the thing to do. They would've killed you," John replied.

"That still doesn't explain why you are here," Simon said. "As far as I know, you aren't with any government-sponsored agency."

"As far as you know," John said.

Simon squinted at him. "You mean you *are* with a government-sponsored agency?"

"I didn't say that."

"What *did* you say?"

"I didn't say anything."

Realizing that he wasn't going anywhere with that, Simon returned to his earlier question. "All right, I'll ask again. What are you doing here?"

"I told you, I'm just passing through," John said. At that moment a Humvee, painted a lusterless gray, came driving across the flowered meadow, moving slowly, but authoritatively, through the midst of the crowd of government, state, and county officials. The driver honked and John started toward it. Simon tried to look inside the Humvee, but the windows were so darkly shaded that it was impossible.

"Who's in the vehicle?" Simon asked.

"See you around, Simon," John replied as he climbed into the Humvee. The driver swung the vehicle around, then drove away. The Humvee went slowly while passing through the crowd, but sped up when it was clear, finally trailing a huge rooster-tail of dust as it left the field and turned onto the small dirt road that led away from the meadow.

Simon watched the Humvee drive away, then took out his phone and started to call the agency number back in Washington. They would know why John Barrone was here. He punched a couple of numbers, then changed his mind. This was a no-win situation. If John Barrone was supposed to be here, Simon would be showing his ignorance by letting headquarters know that he didn't know anything about it. If John Barrone wasn't supposed to be here, Simon's inquiry might cause trouble for him, and he didn't want to do that. After all, John Barrone had probably saved his life today.

And today wasn't the first time Barrone had saved his life.

Simon cleared the numbers, then closed up the phone. Whatever reason Barrone had had for being here was his own business, and Simon had no intention of interfering.

"Who was that?" Muldoon asked, coming up to Simon just after John left.

"Just someone from Washington, checking up on us," Simon lied. "You know how Washington is."

"Yeah, I know. I wish those desk-loving bastards would stay in Washington and keep the hell out of our way. On the other hand, this was a good operation so his report can't hurt us. And I think we've seen the last of these Aryan groups."

"What makes you think so?"

"Because anyone who would join a group like that needs a leader," Muldoon explained. "And with Clendenning gone, there's no one else around."

"Yes, there is."

"Where?"

"He hasn't surfaced yet," Simon said. "But you can bet your bottom dollar that he is out there."

"Who do you think it will be?"

"I have no idea," Simon replied. "But I can describe him for you. He has a confused and misguided soul, but he also has power and charisma. He is probably a born leader, the kind with a warped sense of patriotism. He's the type of person who should be kept locked up during peacetime, but turned loose to lead an army during time of war."

Norton chuckled. "You make him sound a little like General Patton."

"Patton. Yes, he's probably a lot like Patton."

FOUR

Ar Rawdatayn, Kuwait

A Bell 205, painted in desert colors, though with the markings of a civilian oil company, sat on a square of perforated steel planking. One man was fueling the helicopter; another was replacing filters. A Mercedes arrived on the scene, then stopped. Because all the windows of the car, including the windshield, were darkly shaded, it was impossible to see inside the car. As a result, the car, sitting there with its black windows, took on a personality of its own, like the 1958 Plymouth in Stephen King's novel *Christine.*

Brigadier General Arlington Lee Grant of the United States Army was sitting in a pickup truck watching as the helicopter was being fueled. When the car arrived, he got out of the pickup and walked over to it. The driver's-side window slid down silently. When Grant leaned over to look inside, he saw two swarthy-complexioned men.

"Gentlemen," he said.

"You are Rambo?" the driver asked.

"I am." Grant had taken the code name Rambo for the purpose of this meeting. It was, he thought, a little touch of irony probably lost on these two.

"I liked the Rocky movies better," the driver said, surprising Grant by his recognition of the name.

Grant cleared his throat. "Yes, they were good movies," he agreed.

The driver and passenger were Kuwaitis, though they were representing the Allah Freedom Front of Iraq. This was an organization dedicated to overthrowing Saddam Hussein. The Allah Freedom Front did not enjoy the support of the United States, because they were quite candid about their intention of replacing the dictatorship of Saddam Hussein with a dictatorship of their own. They did suggest, however, that their dictatorship would be friendlier to the United States.

To General Grant, a dictatorship friendly to the United States was good enough. He was of the opinion that no country in the Middle East could govern itself anyway, so why not support a friendly dictator?

Then, when he'd realized that neither the Allied military command nor the U.S. State Department was going to listen to his opinion, he'd taken it upon himself to deal with the Allah Freedom Front. His reasoning was that if it was a fait accompli, the U.S. would have no choice but to deal with the new government. Grant planned to do everything within his power to make it a fait accompli.

"You have what I need?" Grant asked.

The driver handed Grant a manila envelope. "You'll find everything in there," the driver said. "Good luck."

Before Grant could even answer, the darkened window slid back up and the car pulled away. Grant stood there for a moment, watching the plume of dust swirl up from behind the Mercedes as it raced across the desert floor.

Grant took the envelope back over to the pickup, then sat in the front seat to open it. Inside, he found a letter of introduction to Mehdi Jahmshedi, the head of the Allah Freedom Front.

The plan was for Mehdi Jahmshedi to have several of his men, wearing uniforms of the Iraqi military, cross into Kuwait and attack one of the oil fields. They would do substantial damage to the oil field, damaging a lot of American property in the process. That would then provide the justification Grant needed to move his men across the border into Iraq. The Allah Freedom Front would then use that opportunity to mount their own attack and, if successful, bring down Saddam Hussein.

The details of the operation had to be worked out in secret, so Grant planned to fly into Iraq to meet with Mehdi Jahmshedi.

Early in his career, Grant had been an Army aviator. His duty as a brigade commander did not require him to fly, but he managed to maintain his proficiency by logging several hours each month.

In order to keep the operation secret, even from the U.S. military, Grant was going to fly a civilian helicopter into Iraq. Mehdi Jahmshedi had connections with some wealthy Kuwaitis. It was the Kuwaitis who had initiated the contact with General Grant, and it was they who'd furnished the helicopter.

The plan called for Grant to take off from Ar Rawdatayn, take up a heading of 295 degrees, and fly approximately one hundred miles across the Kuwait-Iraq border to a point in the desert halfway between Al Busayyah and As Salman. His signal to land would be green smoke. That was where he would meet with Mehdi Jahmshedi.

After a thorough study of all the details, General Grant walked over to the helicopter. The fuel truck had pulled away, and the lone mechanic, also a Kuwaiti, was standing by the right front door.

"All the filters have been changed, and your tanks are full. You have three hours, plus an hour of reserve," the mechanic said. "Also, I've done a thorough preflight. You are ready to go."

"Thanks, but you won't be offended if I do my own preflight?" Grant said.

"If you wish," the mechanic replied, stepping away from the helicopter.

"Oh, I more than wish," Grant said. "I insist."

Using the assist steps, Grant climbed up on top of the helicopter and began examining the pitch-change links, rotor-head, and blades. Then, opening the access panels, he peered into the engine and transmission compartments for a long moment. Finally, he hopped back down and moved to the rear of the helicopter, where he reached up to the tail rotor and cycled it through its pitch changes.

Grant was always thorough with his preflight inspections, but never more so than now, because he would be flying through the no-fly zone. That meant he would be regarded as an intruder to both Coalition and Iraqi forces. Whoever picked him up on radar first would, no doubt, try to shoot him down.

General Grant did have one advantage that not even the Kuwaitis knew about. Because of his position, General Grant had access to the IFF codes that were used by all aircraft flying in the Aircraft Identification Zone. The IFF Codes changed every day according to a schedule published in the Signal Operating Instructions. One had only to check the date and the coordinates in the SOI in order to put in the right codes. Of course, as the SOI was top secret, only a few people had access to it. But as a brigade commander, General Grant was one of those people, and now, as he sat in the helicopter prior to starting it, he programmed his transponder to emit the right codes. The code he chose, however, wasn't a military code, for it would have been to easy to check up on any military aircraft flying in the zone. The code he used would identify his helicopter as a civilian craft, belonging to ARA-CON Oil.

Even with the correct code programmed into his transponder, the operation wasn't risk-free. It would work the first time he was challenged, but it wouldn't hold up for long, especially once he was actually in the no-fly zone. The idea was just to buy enough time to cross the border. Once he was across the border, he would be on his own.

Finished with his preflight and final cockpit check, General Grant strapped himself in, turned on the switches, then with his left index finger pulled the starter trigger, which was located just under the grip of the collective pitch control. Through his earphones, he could hear the igniters snapping as the turbine began to turn. He monitored the N1 and N2 gauges until he was satisfied that he had a good start.

When engine and rotor RPM were stabilized, He pulled up on the collective, causing the helicopter to get light on its skids, adjusted the antitorque pedals, then lifted off the ground.

Within minutes after crossing the Kuwait-Iraq border, his transponder lights started flashing, and General Grant knew he was being painted by radar. Seconds later, he was challenged.

"Aircraft flying on a two-niner-five radial out of Ar Rawdatayn, squawk your parrot."

Grant hit the switch on the transponder, sending out an identification signal.

"You are a civilian aircraft with ARACON Oil?" the radar operator asked, responding to the IFF.

"That's affirmative," Grant replied.

"Sir, you did not file a zone penetration and you have crossed the Iraqi border. Please turn back at once."

"Sorry, I must have gotten a little off course," Grant said. "Executing a one-hundred-eighty-degree turn now."

As Grant started his turn, he also started losing altitude until he was no more than ten feet above the desert floor. This allowed him to drop off the radar screen. Once he was off the screen, he returned to his original heading.

Although one hundred knots is not very fast for an aircraft, the fact that he was only ten feet above the ground gave the illusion of tremendous speed. Small hills of sand, clumps of brown vegetation, rocks and gullies flashed by as he maintained speed, heading, and altitude. Through his headset he could hear the occasional chatter of patrolling Coalition aircraft, and was pleased that, so far at least, he had not been detected.

Just ahead and slightly to his right, Grant saw a column of smoke twisting into a green rope, climbing into the air. He headed for the smoke. When he landed, six armed men approached the aircraft. Grant started to shut down the engine, but something about the menacing appearance of the men gave him second thoughts. He kept the engine running.

"General Grant?" the leader asked. All six men were bearded, but this man had a lot of gray in his beard.

"Yes. Are you Jahmshedi?"

The leader said something to the others, and they all raised their rifles, pointing them at Grant.

"General Grant, you are now a prisoner of the Allah Freedom Front."

"What?" Grant replied in surprise. "What the hell are you doing? I'm on your side, you son of a bitch!"

"We think we can get more from your government if we hold you hostage," Jahmshedi said. "Shut down the engine and get out of the helicopter, please."

"Fuck you."

Jahmshedi spoke again, and this time the others opened fire at the helicopter, not shooting at Grant, but shooting up through the rotor blades. The blades started whistling as wind passed through the bullet holes.

"What's the matter with you?" Grant shouted. "Have you gone crazy?"

"I said shut down the engine and get out of the helicopter," Jahmshedi repeated. "Next time we shoot, we will shoot you."

"All right, all right, I'm shutting down," Grant said.

But instead of shutting down, Grant used the thumb switch on the fuel control to spool up the engine to full takeoff RPM. Just as Jahmshedi noticed the RPM was increasing rather than decreasing, Grant jerked the collective full up. The helicopter leaped from the ground. As it did so, the skid caught Jahmshedi under his chin, knocking him down.

Grant's unexpected action so startled the others that for a moment they were unable to react. This was fortunate, because the helicopter was hanging suspended in the air, like a big balloon. Grant shoved the cyclic forward at about the same time the Iraqis on the ground recovered. They started shooting at him, and electrical sparks flew as bullets popped up through the console. Several of his instruments went dead. Smoke filled the cabin, and he could smell the acrid stench of electrical shorts.

In addition to the shot-up console and instrument panel, the helicopter sustained other damage. There was a severe lateral shimmy, denoting a damaged tail rotor, while bullet holes in the rotor blades were giving him a bad vertical vibration. Almost immediately thereafter, the controls began to stiffen, and he realized that he had also lost hydraulics to his servos. He could still fly, but it was going to be difficult to maintain control . . . far too difficult to fly on the deck as he had coming in.

That opened up new problems, for he was now vulnerable to attack either from Iraqi antiaircraft missiles or from fighter aircraft from one of the Allied nations patrolling the no-fly zone. To make matters worse, his radios and the transponder had been shot out. If challenged, he couldn't even make his case.

Grant couldn't worry about any of that now. He had his hands full just keeping the helicopter in the air. He was so busy, in fact, that he didn't see the two U.S. Navy fighters approaching him from the east.

"Top Hat One, do you have a visual?" a young lieutenant in the Combat Control Center asked.

"Roger," a disembodied voice replied over the speaker. This was Top Hat One, leader of the two F-18 aircraft that had been dispatched when an aircraft in violation of the no-fly zone popped up on the radar screen.

"Can you identify the aircraft?"

"It is a Bell helicopter, with ARACON Oil Company markings," Top Hat One replied.

"Has he responded to any radio messages?"

"Negative."

"Stand by, Top Hat One."

The two F-18's orbited high and behind the helicopter as they awaited further instructions.

Back on the carrier, the operations officer was already in communication with the chief of operations at ARACON Oil.

"You are absolutely positive you don't have any helicopters flying in southern Iraq?" Peterson asked.

"Commander, we only have two helicopters in our inventory and I'm eyeballing both of them right now. I don't know what helicopter your boys are looking at, but it isn't one of ours."

Peterson hung up the phone, then looked at the

young lieutenant. "Have the fighters take him out, Mr. Johnson."

"Sir, are you sure about that?" Johnson asked. "Maybe we should just follow him. I mean, how much damage can a person do in one Bell helicopter?"

"How much damage did a rubber boat do to the U.S.S. *Cole*?" Peterson replied.

Johnson nodded. "Good point, sir." He keyed the microphone. "Top Hat, your authenticator is Grand Slam. I say again, your authenticator is Grand Slam. Take him down."

"Roger that," Top Hat One replied.

As General Grant passed over the border back into Kuwait, he breathed a sigh of relief. If he had to, he could put down almost anywhere now and walk away from this. The whole thing had been an exercise in futility; terrifying, maybe even exciting, but absolutely futile.

Suddenly the inside of the cockpit was filled with a blinding light. Grant felt a blow to the back of the seat, as if he had been rear-ended by a Mack truck. Enunciator lights flashed on, audio signals beeped, and the helicopter began spinning around uncontrollably. As it did a complete 180-degree spin, General Grant saw pieces of his tail-cone falling away. With a sick feeling, he realized that he was now in only one half of an aircraft. He was no longer flying; he was the helpless occupant of a piece of falling wreckage.

FIVE

Falls Church, Virginia

When Arlington Lee Grant answered the doorbell, he was surprised to see Congressman Hugh Anderson, Republican of Texas, and Congresswoman Fala Watson, Democrat of California, standing on his front porch. It wasn't that he was surprised to see a couple of congressmen calling on him; during the ordeal of his trial, he had been visited frequently, both by members of Congress and by members of their staff. But he was very surprised to see these two together.

Anderson was somewhat to the right of Attila the Hun. He'd once tried to introduce a bill that would have disenfranchised anyone whose federal income tax payment from the year before did not meet the national average. In his words, this would "get rid of those welfare recipients and the riffraff who look at government only as a feeding trough. It would also discourage those blacks who have allowed their vote to be corrupted by always voting in a block." Anderson's racist rhetoric often embarrassed even the most conservative members of his party.

Congresswoman Watson was Anderson's exact opposite. She was considerably left of Lenin, a social activist who believed that every African American should receive from the federal government a yearly payment equal to the national average income. This, she claimed, was repayment for the yoke of slavery her people had once endured. She was also quick to defend any outrage committed by any black with the claim that they were driven to do it by that same yoke of slavery. Like Congressman Anderson, Congresswoman Watson's ideology was so far out that she wasn't considered to be a significant voice for her party, or for the liberal cause.

A well-known political columnist once wrote that the idea of Anderson and Watson being in the halls of Congress at the same time filled him with fear. "They are," he suggested, "like matter and antimatter, and if they come into too close a proximity, they could create an event horizon, turning the entire capital into a black hole."

And yet these two members of Congress, without any personal entourage, and without any prior notification, were now standing on the front porch of Arlington Lee Grant's rented house.

"May we come in, General?" Anderson asked.

"I'm sure you realize that I am no longer a general," Grant replied. "I was reduced to colonel and involuntarily retired."

"Yes, a travesty," Anderson said.

Grant stepped away from the door. "Come in," he said. Using his cane, he led his two visitors into his study.

"Are you recovering from your injuries?" Congresswoman Watson asked as she sat on the couch. Anderson settled in a leather chair and Grant sat across from them.

"Yes, only my leg is still bothering me," Grant replied. "And the doctor says even it will heal completely."

"You were very lucky. Not many people could have their helicopter blown out of the sky with an air-to-air missile and walk away," Anderson said. "I saw the pictures of what was left of your helicopter during the congressional hearings."

"The whole world saw the pictures," Grant said. "They tell me that my hearings had a higher rating than the Clinton impeachment. And hell, I didn't even have any sex involved," he added with a cynical laugh.

"Well, you can blame the Administration for the inquisition," Anderson said. "They didn't really want justice. What they wanted was theater."

"In that case, I guess they got what they wanted. I do thank you for coming to my defense during those hearings," Grant said.

"I and all decent Americans were offended by the whole thing," Anderson replied. "You were the finest general on our active roles. And what did you get for taking a little initiative? You were humiliated, reduced in rank, and cashiered from the Army."

Grant wasn't surprised that Anderson had been one of his strongest defenders during the hearings. Grant and Anderson shared a political philosophy. Even while he was still on active duty, General Grant had been an ultraconservative who spoke often and publicly about his beliefs. His willingness to do so had often caused controversy, and he had received several reminders from the Department of Defense that a person of his rank was expected to keep a lower profile.

"I don't believe you share that view, do you, Congresswoman Watson?" Grant asked.

"I don't share that view at all, General. I think what you did was more than take a little initiative," Congresswoman Watson said. "You attempted to usurp a responsibility that belongs solely to Congress. In my opinion, you were trying to declare war on Iraq."

"You're damn right I was," Grant said. "But surely you didn't come here to continue the debate?"

"No," Watson said quickly. "I certainly did not."

"Then why are you here?"

"We came here to call upon your personal patriotism," Anderson said.

"You'll forgive me if I don't feel particularly patriotic toward the government right now," Grant replied.

Anderson chuckled.

"What's so funny?"

"We aren't interested in your patriotism toward the government," Congresswoman Watson explained. "We are more concerned in your patriotism toward the people."

"The people?"

"Yes, the people," Anderson agreed.

Grant stared at the two of them for a long, silent moment. Then he got up and limped over to the liquor cabinet, where he opened a door and took out a bottle. "I normally like a little bourbon about this time of day," he said. He held the bottle up. "Could I interest either of you in a bit of the creature?"

"A little bourbon and branch, if you don't mind," Anderson said.

"And I'll take mine neat," Watson added.

Grant poured the drinks, then returned to the seating area.

"Okay, so we are all bourbon drinkers," he said. "At least we share that." He handed them the drinks. "But I sure as hell don't see what else we have in common. You are calling upon me to show my patriotism for the people. But I can't believe that means the same thing to each of you."

Anderson and Watson looked at each other exchanging, not a smile, but a nod of understanding.

"You've got that part right," Anderson said. "We don't have the same interests, we don't represent the same agenda. In fact, we agree upon only one thing, and that is what we are against."

"And what are you against?"

"We are against the government," Watson explained.

"And in that, we can find a common ground, for our hate and distrust in the present government is wide, deep, and significant enough to make us unholy allies," Anderson added.

"And yet you are both representatives of the government you profess to hate. Why is that? Are you trying to change it from within?"

"We have come to the mutual decision that changing the government from within is not possible," Anderson said. "She is pushing one way and I am pushing the other. Under such conditions, the best we could ever hope for is a complete stalemate."

"That's why we need you," Watson said.

Grant shook his head and held out his hands. "If you are wanting me to make some futile run for President, like Buchanan, or Nader, or Perot, forget it. I never do battle unless there is some chance to win."

"We don't want you to run for President," Watson said. "That would accomplish nothing."

"Then what do you want?"

"We want this government terminated," Anderson said.

"Terminated?"

"Overthrown," Watson explained.

Grant looked at them as if he couldn't believe what he'd just heard. Then he let out a long sigh.

"Well, now, that's a rather sizable order, isn't it? And with what would you replace our current government?"

"With a government that is weighted in such a way as to allow full and equal sharing of power by African Americans," Watson said.

"With a government that guarantees the rights of

the white Christians who founded this country," Anderson put in.

Grant looked at the two of them with a confused look on his face, then shook his head. "Have you two gone stark raving mad? Those goals are diametrically opposed."

"They are, and we accept that," Anderson replied. "But we do believe that before either of us can work toward our goal, we must eliminate the biggest obstacle that is before us."

"Which we believe is the United States government," Watson added.

"Once the current government is crushed, there will be a vacuum. For the moment, our mutual goal is the dissolution of the current government. We think we can work together toward that end," Anderson said.

"However, once the current government is gone, we will revert to our individual agendas. Those I represent will try, in every way possible, to fill the vacuum with new, more socially active programs," Watson said.

"And we will try just as hard to put our program into place," Anderson added.

"My God. You are calling for a civil war," Grant said.

"Not exactly," Anderson said. "Though of course, with the collapse of the government, there will be some rending of the social fabric, perhaps some unrest in the streets. But there will be no real battles. Ultimately, I believe there will be a realignment of borders, and America will become in reality what it already is in fact. Two nations, one white, and one black. We, of course, will be the larger, more dominant nation."

"You agree with that logic?" Grant asked Congresswoman Watson.

"Yes," Watson replied. "I don't believe the division

of power will be quite as one-sided as Congressman Anderson envisions. The nation I would be associated with would be much more inclusive than his, and as I am sure you are aware, the total number of minority citizens, to include all peoples of color, not just African Americans, is rapidly approaching half the population of the United States."

"The bottom line is, we think those details can be worked out, once we accomplish our first goal," Anderson concluded.

"You understand, don't you, Miss Watson, that I, personally, tend to ally myself more with Congressman Anderson's ideas than I do with yours."

"Yes. But as they say, political expediency makes strange bedfellows. For the time being, we all have the same goal, the destruction of the government," Watson replied.

"And you can help us achieve that goal," Anderson added.

"I took an oath to preserve and defend the Constitution of the United States," Grant said sharply.

"And you have done so admirably, in Vietnam, during the Gulf War, in Bosnia, and more recently with the peacekeepers in Iraq," Anderson said. "And how were you repaid for your loyalty?"

"I hold no rancor for the Department of Defense," Grant replied. "They recommended nonjudicial punishment, which would have allowed me to keep my rank and quietly retire."

"But Congress wouldn't allow that," Anderson said. "They hauled you before the Armed Services Committee for public humiliation."

"I know you and I have our differences, General Grant, but Congressman Anderson and I agree that as a result of what happened to you, you have been released from your oath of commission."

"Okay, suppose you are right," Grant said. "And suppose I agree to help. What is next?"

"Have you ever heard of an organization called The Shield?" Anderson asked.

"The Shield?" Grant shook his head. "No, I can't say as I have."

"They made a lot of news last year, but it's understandable if you haven't heard of them. You've been on active duty out of the country for a while," Anderson said.

"What is The Shield?"

"They were an organization on the outer edge of the right wing."

Grant nodded. "Wait a minute, yes, I know who you are talking about. A man and his wife were the head of it. Clendenning? Something like that?"

"Luke Clendenning. He, his wife, and eight of their followers were killed, but their martyrdom has had a very positive effect. Clendenning has become almost an icon to the white supremacists. He is much more popular in death than he ever was in life."

"What does that have to do with me?"

"We want you to become the new Luke Clendenning," Watson said.

Grant chuckled. "Thanks, but no, thanks. I have no wish to become a martyr."

"We don't mean that," Anderson explained hastily. "What we want is for you to step into the leadership vacuum. There are several conservative political and militia groups around the country. We believe you have the stature to draw them all under one umbrella."

Grant took another swallow of his drink, then studied his two visitors over the rim of his glass. He looked at Watson. "I'm still having a hard time coming to grips with your involvement in this," he said. "Why have you come to me? Why don't you go to one of your own people?"

"Because we don't have your counterpart in our society," Watson replied. "Our leaders tend to have more of a religious background than a military background. You not only have the military background, you also have the stature to attract people to your cause."

"All right, I can see that," Grant agreed.

"We want you to become the head of Freedom Nation," Anderson said.

"What is Freedom Nation? I've never heard of it."

"No such group exists as yet," Anderson admitted. "But we believe you have the leadership, organizational skills, and charisma to start it."

"And how am I supposed to do this? By turning out mimeographed broadsheets?"

"Heavens, no," Watson replied. "With proper use of the Internet, you can make your presence known right away."

"And we are prepared to give you one million dollars for organization and recruitment expenses," Anderson concluded.

"I'll be my own boss," Grant said. "I don't want to have to answer to either of you."

"Believe me, this is the last contact you'll ever have with me," Congresswoman Watson said. "I'm sure you can understand that neither of us can afford to be seen together."

"And you?" Grant asked Anderson.

"Once you agree to do it, and take the money, you'll hear nothing more from me," Anderson promised.

"What about Coldfire?" Watson asked.

"Yes, except for Coldfire. When the time comes, I will contact you about Coldfire."

"What is Coldfire?"

"As a military man, I am sure you are aware of the concept 'Need to know,' " Anderson said.

"Yes, of course."

"You will be filled in on Coldfire when you have the need to know."

SIX

Moscow, Russia

In front of the Sandunov Baths in downtown Moscow, a middle-aged man leaned against the side of his battered old Zhiguli. The car, once a proud possession, had like its owner seen better days. The Zhiguli had been lime green when it was new, and that was still the predominant color, though the crumpled left front fender was painted in a gray primer, and the right rear door was laced with an orange-brown rust. Two of the windows were broken, and the tailpipe emitted a smoke screen when it was being driven because the engine used oil badly. However, the car was serviceable enough to function as a taxi, and despite the fact that he was forbidden by Army regulations to operate a private taxi service, that was exactly what he was doing.

As he waited, Colonel Yuri Shaporin puffed on a cheap Prima cigarette. Since the fall of Communism, the rise of democracy, and Russia's new accord with the West, Moscow's stores and shops were filled with many wonderful things. Products that could only have been dreamed about by the average Soviet citizen in the past were now available in great quantity. The Russian consumer was assailed with such goods as VCRs, McDonald's hamburgers, ballpoint pens, and American cigarettes.

Yuri thought of the irony of the situation. Before the collapse of the Soviet Union he'd had money, but there had been few things available for him to buy. Now the stores' windows and shelves were filled to overflowing, but Yuri no longer had money. The cheap Prima cigarette smoke filled his mouth with a powerful and bitter taste, but he smoked them because even a single pack of American cigarettes was beyond his means.

It wasn't always that way. Yuri had graduated with honors from the prestigious Frunze Military Academy, and had done exceptionally well in the Army. In 1980 Yuri, then a lieutenant, was part of the Soviet Olympic Team. His event was the individual pentathlon, the military event of riding, fencing, shooting, swimming, and running. Yuri won the bronze medal, taking first place in shooting and running. He would have won the gold had the horse he was given not balked at every obstacle, causing him to come in last in a field of thirty-three in the riding event.

There was never any doubt as to whether or not Yuri would serve in the Army. His father had been a major general during World War II, or as the Russians called it, the Great Patriotic War. Major General Shaporin had successfully led his 20th Army in a counterattack against General Heinz Guderian's 112th Division, causing the Germans to break and run. That was the first time since the invasion of Russia that the German Army had been turned back, and the drive on Moscow had been stopped. For that, Josef Stalin had personally decorated General Shaporin with the award of Hero of the Soviet Union. Yuri's father was dead now, but he had lived long enough to see his son win a commission.

Colonel Shaporin also had combat experience, having been decorated during the Soviet war in Afghanistan. Yuri pulled the cigarette out and pinched the end off with his fingers. He dropped the butt into his pocket so that later he could use the tobacco in a pipe. He thought about Afghanistan; a lost war waged by forgotten men, serving the failed ideology of a now-defunct nation.

Colonel Shaporin was still on active duty in the Russian military. He was the commander of a tactical-missile battalion in the Tamansky Motorized Infantry Division in an Army camp just outside Moscow. How well he could remember the halcyon days when, during the May Day parades, he would lead his battalion through Red Square. How proud he'd been of the missiles on display, the motorized launchers glistening, the tough, well-disciplined soldiers marching proudly, the crowd cheering, the leaders of the Soviet Union staring down, the entire world watching and, most of all, fearing the Army of the Soviet Union.

But that was no more.

Now his missiles had had their warheads removed and stored, and of the twenty-two motorized launchers in his command, only two would run; though they never did so because of the lack of gasoline. It was a sad state of affairs for what had once been a great Army. The entire Tamansky Division presented the same bleak picture of vehicles rusting in motor parks without repair parts or fuel, and of barracks with collapsed roofs, broken windows, and no coal to heat them. The mess halls served only two meals per day: a coarse-grained black bread and coffee for breakfast, and the same fare again for dinner, though augmented with a piece of cheese or a thin soup.

The men who had once worn their uniforms so proudly were now deserting at a rate higher than fifty percent. Yuri knew that none of them had been paid in over three months, because he hadn't. It was for that reason that he, the perfect soldier, was now violating Army regulations to earn some money by using his car as a taxi.

Yuri's wife and three children, who during the good years had lived in senior officers' quarters, attended to by well-mannered orderlies and enjoying all the perks of a colonel in the Soviet military, now lived in a tiny three-room apartment, barely getting enough to eat.

But that might all change. It depended on what happened at his meeting today, a meeting that had been set up by an event that had occurred yesterday.

Yesterday, Yuri had picked up a fare. The passenger, who looked well fed, was wearing an expensive suit and a gold watch. He gave the address, then leaned back in his seat. In his rearview mirror, Yuri saw that the man was studying him.

"Good day to you, Colonel Shaporin," the passenger finally said.

Yuri felt a moment of panic. How did his passenger know him? Was he a military policeman, about to arrest Yuri for taking a part-time job in violation of Army regulations?

"I must tell you, you did not pick me up by chance. I planned this meeting," the passenger said.

Yuri sighed. "I can explain why I'm working. I have not been paid in many months. I have a family, and . . ."

The passenger laughed. "Relax, Colonel, relax. I am not with the police. Don't you recognize me?"

Yuri studied him more closely. "Should I know you?" he asked.

"Perhaps not. Our ranks are too far apart. I am Andrei Glizkov, one-time Corporal Andrei Glizkov." Glizkov chuckled. "I suppose that technically I am still Corporal Glizkov, since I have never been officially discharged."

"You are a deserter?" Yuri asked.

"In a manner of speaking, I suppose I am."

"You are a deserter, and you have the effrontery to ride in my cab?" Yuri asked angrily.

"Take it easy, Colonel. Neither of us would want to encounter a military policeman at this point, would we?"

Yuri knew that Glizkov was right. He could not turn his passenger in without getting into trouble. He was angry for allowing himself to be put into such a position.

"Colonel, aren't you interested in why I chose your cab?" Glizkov asked.

"So you could bait me?" Yuri snapped back.

"No, Colonel. So I could help you."

"What could you possibly do to help me?" Yuri asked.

"Actually, I should say, so we could help each other," Glizkov replied. "Colonel, have you noticed how I am dressed?"

"I hadn't paid any attention," Yuri lied.

"The suit I am wearing costs more money than you make in one year. The watch would take two years of your salary. That is, when the Army *pays* your salary," he added with a sneer. "You have not been paid for three months, have you?"

"That is none of your concern," Yuri replied.

"But it does concern me . . . to see our heroes so mistreated," Glizkov said. "I, on the other hand, have a great deal of money. Do you not wonder how I came by it?"

"I'm sure it isn't honest," Yuri said.

"Honest? What is honest?" Glizkov asked, laughing. "Colonel, you are still thinking like a socialist. We live in a capitalist country now. There is opportunity for everyone, if they understand the system."

"And you understand the system?"

"I understand the system very well," Glizkov said. "And I can teach it to you." He leaned over the backseat. "Even though I am a deserter, I am not a man without honor. Colonel, you were my commander during the war in Afghanistan and I still feel a great loyalty toward you. That is why I am giving you this opportunity."

"What opportunity?"

"An opportunity to make fifty thousand dollars in U.S. currency. Do you have any idea how much money fifty thousand U.S. dollars is? At the current rate of exchange, that is well over one million rubles."

"One million?" Yuri gasped at the amount, and looked around so abruptly that he didn't see the bus in front of him.

"Colonel, the bus!" Glizkov shouted in alarm.

Yuri slammed on the brakes, and the Zhiguli skidded to a halt inches short of the bus. In the windows of the bus he could see the passengers' faces, and their expressions of surprise, fear, and anger at the near miss. With a sigh of relief for having avoided the accident, Yuri pulled to the side of the street, then stopped. Safely out of the traffic, he twisted around to look at his passenger.

"What would I have to do for that kind of money?" he asked.

"Be in front of the Sandunov Baths at fifteen hours tomorrow," Glizkov said. "You will be met by a German businessman named Otto Maass."

"And?"

"Herr Maass will make you a business proposition," Glizkov said. "If you are smart, you will take him up on his offer."

"What sort of business proposition?"

"That is not for me to say, Colonel. Oh, you can let me out here."

"This isn't your destination."

"That's all right. My car is following," Glizkov said,

paying with a bill that was twice the amount of the fare, then exiting the car without waiting for change.

Yuri watched in his mirror as Glizkov got into the late-model Zil that had been following them.

That had all happened yesterday. It was now five minutes after three and Yuri had been at his appointed place for ten minutes. He was about to believe that his old corporal was playing a cruel joke on him, and had turned to open the door of his car, when a glistening limousine pulled to the curb.

He couldn't help but be impressed by the car, a late-model Mercedes. Yuri couldn't even imagine how much a Mercedes must cost in Russia.

Yuri watched as the chauffeur hurried around to open the rear door of the car. An old man slid out of the backseat.

"Ah, Colonel Shaporin, you are here, I see," the man said, smiling at Yuri.

"You are Herr Maass?"

"Yes. Come inside with me, won't you? We will take the baths and get acquainted."

Inside the *banya*, the foyer was decorated with plaster cherubs and rococo murals. A stoic old *babushka*, oblivious of the naked men around her, collected the price of admission.

"I am an international businessman, Colonel, and wherever I go, I enjoy the local customs," Maass said. "In America they have something called a barbecue, which I like very much. In Japan, it's the geisha. They are not prostitutes, you know. And here, in Russia, I like to take the baths." Maass paid for both of them. "Are you a devotee of the baths, Colonel?"

"Not as much as I used to be," Yuri replied.

"No, I imagine the baths are one of those unnecessary expenses you had to eliminate. Too bad, though.

The baths renew one's soul. I believe Glizkov mentioned a possible business arrangement between us?"

"Yes," Yuri answered. "But he didn't say what it was about."

"No, of course not. That is for us to discuss."

From the foyer, the two men walked through the *mylnaya* or washing room. Dozens of naked men of varied ages, social stations, and physical appearances languished along the side of the pool or splashed through the cold water. Maass was right when he'd said this was one of the luxuries Yuri had had to eliminate. In better days, the baths were the domain of senior Army officers, the party elite, and bureaucrats, and he had come often. But now the cost of admission could provide a meal for his family. Nevertheless, he was experienced enough not to be self-conscious about removing his clothes in the wood-paneled dressing room. Naked, he and Maass stepped into the *parilnya*, or steam room. When they entered, there were three men already there, but as if by some prior agreement, they all exited, leaving Yuri and his host alone.

There was a hiss of steam as Maass poured a bucket of water onto the hot stones. Then he and Yuri used birch twigs in vigorous self-flagellation as a type of purification. They climbed to the top bench, where most of the heat was gathered, and sat there for a long moment before Maass finally spoke.

"Colonel, I believe our mutual friend mentioned a sum of fifty thousand American dollars to you?"

"Yes."

"And you are interested, because you are here." It wasn't a question, it was a declaration.

"I would be lying if I said I wasn't interested. But I wonder if I am who you think I am. I mean, what could I possibly do for you that would be worth so much money?"

"Let me tell you what I know about you," Maass

replied. "You command a battalion in the Tamansky Motorized Infantry Division. Your battalion has twenty-two mobile missile-launching vehicles, with two missiles per vehicle. That is a total of forty-four missiles. The missiles have three warheads of five kilotons each. That is one hundred thirty-two warheads."

Without waiting for a reply from Yuri, Maass moved down the row of benches to pour more water onto the hot stones. He was enveloped by the billowing cloud of steam his action caused. Then a moment later, he reemerged as he climbed back up and took his seat beside Yuri. Not until then did he resume the conversation.

"Now, while that sounds impressive, I know also that only two of your vehicles will run. You have neither heat nor food for your men. They have not been paid for some time, and the desertion rate is so high that, if you were mobilized tomorrow, I doubt that you could respond with much more than one company."

"I can explain that," Yuri started defensively.

"You don't have to explain it, Colonel. I understand the situation perfectly. Your entire Army is in just as sorry a state. Your Navy's ships lie at anchor, their crews deserted or drunk, while the rusting hulls leak nuclear waste into the water. The terrible tragedy of the submarine *Kurz*, going down as it did with all hands, can be traced directly to the criminal negligence of your government. Tell me you have not had such thoughts."

"I have had such thoughts," Yuri admitted. "Herr Maass, where are you going with all this?"

"Two weeks from now you will receive orders to dismantle the warheads from your SS-21 missiles and ship them, by train, to a place where they will be destroyed."

"How do you know this? I haven't heard anything about it."

"It will happen."

"But . . . without the warheads, the missiles are useless," Yuri said. "With useless missiles, there is no mission. And if there is no mission, what will become of my battalion?"

"Your battalion will be demobilized, and you will be discharged."

Yuri was silent for a moment. "My pension?"

Maass laughed. "Colonel, you are not being paid now and you are on active service. What makes you think you will get your pension?"

"What will I do? How will I support my family?"

"You can do business with me. Think, Colonel, what you could do with over a million rubles. You could provide the comfortable life for your family that they have every right to expect."

"What do you want from me?"

"One nuclear warhead."

"Impossible. Even if what you say is true, if the battalion is to be demobilized, there will be a strict accounting of all the warheads."

"Not to worry," Maass said. "I will arrange for the inventory to reflect that all warheads were surrendered."

"You can do that? How?"

Maass chuckled. "With money, Colonel. Welcome to the world of capitalism."

SEVEN

The floor director held up his hand. "Coming out of commercial break in ten," he said.

General Grant adjusted his shirt collar and waited. The red light on the middle camera blinked on.

"Welcome back to *Riposte*," the moderator said in a cultivated "This is my profession" voice. "I am Richard Bin-Garon, and my guest is the very controversial retired Colonel Arlington Lee Grant. Colonel Grant, you have been quoted as saying that if the President of the United States had served under you, you would have busted him to private and put him in the brig for incompetence. And yet the President is your commander in chief, is he not? Doesn't such a statement by you put you in violation of military regulations?"

"I'm sure you know, Mr. Bin-Garon, that I am no longer in the Army. I was forced by that unqualified pretender who sits in the White House, and his equally incompetent government, into early retirement. You may have seen it on television," he added dryly.

"Yes, along with millions of Americans. But isn't it true that, unlike the average civilian, a person who is on the retired rolls is still subject to certain standards of military behavior? And if so, one of those standards surely must be that you cannot call the President of the United States an incompetent."

"I can and I do call him that, because that is exactly

what he is. By his total inadequacy for the job he holds, he has brought our nation to the brink of ruin. I would welcome any attempt by the government to bring me to trial. They won't, of course, because they don't want the rest of the world to hear what questions I might ask."

"And what questions would those be, General?"

Grant looked directly at the camera. "For one thing, I would ask about the slaughter of Lucas Clendenning, his wife, and followers at Sky Meadow. They were nothing more than a politically active group of men and women who were exercising their right to live their own lives."

"Luke Clendenning and his group were responsible for the bombing of a children's center in Dallas. That bombing killed several innocent children," Bin-Garon said.

"They are alleged to have been responsible. There is no proof of that. They were never brought to trial."

"They could have been brought to trial if Clendenning had surrendered when he had the opportunity. According to all reports, Clendenning was given that chance when he was confronted at Sky Meadow. But he resisted arrest, violently, and he, his wife, and several of his followers were killed in the ensuing fight. Incidentally, several government agents were killed in that same fight. Surely you can't refer to that as a slaughter. Clendenning was a criminal of the worst sort."

"Perhaps you see him that way. But to me, and to others who believe as I do, Lucas Clendenning will go down in history as a true American hero. We place him on the same level as Patrick Henry, John Adams, and Nathan Hale."

Bin-Garon chuckled snidely. "I'm not sure how Patrick Henry, John Adams, and Nathan Hale would react to being compared to someone like Lucas Clendenning. They were heroes, not racists."

"On the contrary, sir. Those men, indeed *all* of our Founding Fathers, were what the liberals today would consider racists."

"I will confess that there was somewhat less sensitivity for the rights of minorities then, but how do you say they were racists?"

"Understand, Mr. Bin-Garon, that in my lexicon racist is not a pejorative term. On the contrary, it is a term of honor. This country was founded *by* white Christians, *for* white Christians. Indeed, every advancement made in the history of our nation has been made by Aryan Christian men and women. And it is only since our government began a systematic mongrelization of our race that our country has begun to deteriorate, both morally and spiritually."

Bin-Garon looked stunned. "You actually believe that, don't you?"

"I do. That's why I started Freedom Nation. It is built upon the principles and ideals espoused by Lucas Clendenning and his group, the Shield. We will complete the mission Mr. Clendenning started."

"And what exactly is that mission?"

"Restoration of the rights of white Christian Americans."

"How do you propose to do that?"

"By whatever means are necessary."

"I must admit, Colonel, I can't believe I am hearing this from a man like you, a much-decorated combat veteran."

"Someone has to take the initiative," Grant replied. "And I am prepared by training and disposition to be the one who will do that. We must all remember that freedom is not free, and it is not without risk." Grant looked at the camera. "I would like to invite everyone who is concerned about the direction our country is going to join me in this crusade. You can find out more about it by going to *www.freedomnation.com.*"

"Is your invitation open to everyone?" Bin-Garon asked. "Or just white Christians?"

Grant fixed Bin-Garon with a cold glare.

"I don't think Negroes, Hispanics, Asians, Arabs, Jews, or Hindus would feel very comfortable in our group."

"I'm sure you realize, Colonel, that I am Jewish," Bin-Garon said.

"Would you be comfortable with us?"

"I would not."

Grant smiled. "Then you've made my point."

Virginia, a truckstop on I-95

Simon Mason emptied nearly half a bottle of hot sauce on his french fries, then pointed to the booth behind John Barrone. "Would you hand me that hot sauce?"

"Damn," John said, reaching for the new bottle. "You sure you don't want a straw? You could just suck the sauce out."

"These frozen processed french fries don't have any flavor," Simon answered. "You have to doctor them up a little." He started applying the sauce again. "I never did get the chance to thank you for saving my ass back in Sky Meadow. A couple of more rounds from those recoilless rifles, and we would have been history."

"Glad to be of help."

"You aren't on any agency's payroll, are you?" Simon asked as he forked several coated french fries to his mouth.

"What makes you think I'm not?"

"I did some checking. If you are official, you're so

deep I can't find you. And I'm good at my job, John. If I can't find you, nobody can, which tells me you are outside the system. If I'm wrong, say something right now, and we'll just have a nice meal together; then when it's over, you go your way and I'll go mine."

John took a swallow of his coffee, but didn't say anything.

"That's what I thought," Simon said. "And that's what I hoped. Because what I've got won't survive the system. There are too many political appointees in critical positions, and I don't know who can be trusted and who can't. Shall I go on?"

"I'm listening," John said.

That was exactly what Simon wanted to hear, and the expression on his face reflected his relief.

"What do you know about General Arlington Lee Grant? Well, Colonel, retired, now."

"Only what I've seen on television and read in the papers," John said. "He got into some trouble over in Iraq. He managed to avoid a court-martial, but the House Armed Services Committee hauled him up for a hearing. Actually, I think he got a raw deal. I think we should help Iraqi dissidents overthrow Saddam Hussein."

"I must confess, he had my sympathy then too," Simon said. "But have you followed any of his activity since then?"

"Not really. I know he's been a guest on a few television talk shows. Defending his action, I guess. I've not watched any of them."

"You should have," Simon said. "The man has gone off the deep end."

"How so?"

"For one thing, he is carrying on where Lucas Clendenning left off."

"You mean bombing children's centers?"

"I don't know that he has done anything like that

yet," Simon said. "But I do know that he has started an organization that is modeled on The Shield. He calls his group Freedom Nation."

"What have they done?"

"So far, nothing. But there is something in the wind, something big."

"What?"

Simon finished his french fries, then leaned back in his seat and stared across the table at John. "I wish to hell I knew the answer to that question," he said. "All I know is, he has been in contact with several international arms dealers."

"Has he bought anything?"

"If so, he hasn't taken delivery. And because he hasn't taken delivery, he is not in violation of the Sullivan Act, or anything else we can get him on. So far all he has done is spread a lot of hate talk around, and for that, he is protected by the First Amendment."

"You don't think it will stop there?"

"No, I don't. He is surrounding himself with combat veterans, men who have served with him in the past. Add to that a pretty active recruitment program, and he is putting together a mercenary unit that could be a serious threat."

"What do your people say about it?"

"They say that until he violates some law, we have no authority to move."

"Simon, you can't go after someone just because his politics might be a little too conservative for you. Hell, I'm conservative. For all I know, I might agree with some of his ideas."

"I know this man, John. I've studied him. He isn't going to make a move until he is ready, and then we won't be able to stop him short of calling out the military. And we can't do that because the Posse Comitatus Act specifically prohibits the use of the military in civil actions."

"Why are you coming to me with this, Simon?"

Simon moved his empty french-fries plate to one side, put his elbows on the table, clasped his hands together, and leaned forward.

"I don't know who you are with, or what the scope of your authority is," Simon said quietly. "As a matter of fact, I'm not sure you have any authority whatever, which might be good, because it also means you have no restrictions. Someone damn well better look into what Grant is doing, and something tells me that you may be the only one who can. Now, the question is, if you are not with any governmental agency, how are you compensated? I mean, would I have to come up with some sort of payment?"

John drummed his fingers on the table for a moment before he answered.

"Did you see the movie *The Godfather*?"

"Yes. I saw it. It was a good movie," Simon said, a little confused by the question.

"You remember when someone came to the Godfather and asked for a favor? He granted it willingly, but reminded the person that, someday, *he* might need a favor."

Simon smiled broadly, then leaned back in his seat again. "Whatever favor I can grant you, Godfather, I will," he said.

Frankfurt, Germany

Otto Maass left his Mercedes in the parking lot at Flughafen Frankfurt Main, waited for a shuttle bus to pass, then crossed the street to the entrance of Terminal 1. Otto was six feet tall, with silver hair and light-blue eyes. Nearly sixty, he had an athletic build, which was accented by his militarily erect carriage.

Women found Otto good-looking in a Prussian sort

of way, and had he been born twenty-five years earlier, he would have been the model for Hitler's Aryan race. In fact, Otto's father, whom Otto resembled, had been an Obergruppenführer in the SS, and once several years ago, Otto, out of curiosity, had tried on his father's uniform. When he looked at himself in the mirror, at the black and silver tunic, the array of medals, and the red swastika armband, he'd felt a strange stirring within. He knew the attraction was unholy, but as he thought of his father, a principal actor upon the stage of the twentieth century's greatest drama, he felt a sense of pride, which he knew he could share with no one.

Otto had been a captain in the postwar German Army, but it was a service obligation only. He'd never had any intention of making the military a career. He wasn't particularly interested in politics either, though he tended to vote conservative. What interested him most was money, and he had been exceptionally successful in pursuit of that goal. Otto was in the "import-export" business. What made his business so successful was the merchandise he handled. Otto specialized in international arms dealing.

For the most part Otto's business was legitimate, for he was a highly respected conduit of Germany's weapons trade. And if sometimes he violated a quota here, or made a slight alteration in a trade agreement there, government officials tended to look the other way. And why shouldn't they? Competition with the other arms-exporting countries—England, France, Russia, and especially the United States—was fierce, and if a German citizen couldn't go to his own country for help, where could he go? Besides, international arms dealing was one of the best ways to maintain a balance of trade.

Not all of the people who looked the other way were acting out of a sense of obligation to their country's economic well-being. Some of them did so because Otto paid them handsomely, especially if what he wanted was too far outside the limits to accommodate a pass from the government. Just how far Otto could get his particular contacts to expand the parameters was about to be put to the extreme test, for today Otto would be accepting delivery of a very special container from Russia. The container would be in his possession only for as long as it would take to off-load it from the Aeroflot plane from Moscow and put it onto a Lufthansa flight for Buenos Aires. Otto had paid a considerable amount of money for the item that was so carefully packed in the container, and because of the extreme sensitivity of the shipment, he was going to have to pay a great deal to ensure that the container left Frankfurt as scheduled. It was an extremely risky operation, but if he could carry it off, the economic reward would be enormous.

When Otto stepped into the club lounge on the ninth floor of the Frankfurt Airport Center, he wasn't even asked to show a card. The maitre d' recognized him at once, and smiled obsequiously as he hurried over to welcome him.

"Ah, Herr Maass, it is good to see you again."

"*Guten haben*, Hans. Is anyone at my table?"

"I can check for you," Hans answered. "If it is occupied, would you like another table?"

"No, I would prefer to wait for my regular," Otto replied.

Hans excused himself, and Otto waited just beyond the red-felt rope, which set the lounge area off from the entry foyer. Stepping over to the window, he watched a Lufthansa 757 climbing out of Frankfurt at a very sharp angle, the noise of its engines reaching his ears in a subdued roar. Four Americans, deeply involved in conversation, came into the club. Otto spoke and understood English well enough to recognize their accents as midwestern.

"You're sure we can come in here, Fred?" one of the women asked. "It would be awfully embarrassing if they kicked us out."

"They damn well better let us in," Fred replied. "I've got about a million miles flyin' first-class. Hell, I'm welcome in ever' first-class lounge in the world."

"I don't know, Fred," the other man said hesitantly. I noticed that the sign outside said, 'Frankfurt Airport Club members only.' Maybe this is something different. We don't have to wait in here. There are other first-class lounges in the terminal."

"No, by God, we're going to wait here. They'll let us in, you'll see."

Hans returned then. "Your table will be ready in just a moment, Herr Maass," he said. "The waiter is clearing it now." Not until then did Hans turn his attention to the four Americans. *"Bitte?"* he asked.

As Otto knew he would, Fred spoke for them. "My wife and my friends and I have a two o'clock flight, first-class, on American Airlines. We'd like to wait in here, if it would be all right."

"This is a private club, sir. Are you a member?"

"Friend, maybe you didn't hear me. I said we are flying first-class. That lets us into any passenger area in the world."

"You said American Airlines, sir? You might try the Admirals Club. It's in Terminal One, between Departures Hall B and C, on the mezzanine."

"I *know* where the Admirals Club is, friend. I want to wait in here," Fred said resolutely.

"Hans," Otto said, "I would appreciate it if you would allow our American visitors in as my guests."

"Ja wohl, Herr Maass," Hans said with a slight bow.

The Americans looked over at Otto in surprise.

"Well, friend . . . Maass, did he call you?" Fred asked. "That's damned decent of you. Thank you."

"You are welcome," Otto replied. "I hope you enjoyed your stay in our country."

"Oh, yes, we had a wonderful time," Fred's wife said. She looked at Otto with an intensity that suggested that at another time, and under different circumstances, she could be approachable.

"This way, please," Hans said, opening the rope to show the Americans through.

"I thank you again, friend," Fred called as Hans led them away. Fred's wife sent one more smoldering gaze in his direction.

Otto watched Hans take them back to a table situated in the far corner, away from any view, very near the service elevator, and he smiled. That was Hans's way of expressing his disapproval of anyone who would circumvent the rules.

Otto had been waiting about five minutes when a small bald-headed man, with rimless glasses and a closely cropped moustache, approached the table. Eugen Brandt was in the gray-green uniform of a customs official, complete with a gold medallion, which denoted twenty years of service.

"Bier, bitte," Brandt said to the waiter as he sat across the table from Otto. Brandt gave the order authoritatively for he was an airport official and the waiter was an airport employee on the lowest tier.

"Ja wohl," the waiter answered with the slightest suggestion of a bowed head.

Otto didn't particularly like Eugen Brandt. Brandt was a mid-level administrator who, outside of his airport fiefdom, would hardly be noticed. He was, Otto thought, the archetypal German bureaucrat, the type who gave Germans a bad name because of the Prussian-like exercise of their limited authority. Although Brandt's authority had a limited effect on the public at large, it had a great impact upon Otto's ability to do business. This was especially so when he had a shipment as sensitive as the one he was dealing with today.

On the other hand, Brandt could be, and had been, bought. And in a strange way, even though it was vital to Otto's operation that Brandt be bought, the fact that he could made Otto dislike the little civil servant even more for the hypocrite he was.

"I'm sorry I was late," Brandt apologized, though Otto knew that it wasn't a genuine apology. It was merely a way of letting Otto know what a busy and important man he was dealing with, and Brandt validated Otto's thought with his next comment. "I had to refuse entry to a shipment of computers from the United States. It caused the most terrible row."

"What was wrong?"

"They had the 28–b shipping forms. The new forms are 1311–a. The shippers should have known that. Notification of the change in forms went out to everyone quite some time ago."

"Isn't the information on both forms the same?" Otto asked.

"Yes."

"Then I don't understand. Why didn't you let them in?"

"Because the forms have changed," Brandt said, as if that explained everything.

Otto started to ask why Brandt didn't just let them fill out the new forms here in the airport instead of refusing entry to the shipment, but he let the question pass. Why bother? Whether or not the computers were allowed in meant nothing to him. Getting his shipment out today meant everything.

"So," Brandt said, accepting the beer from the waiter without so much as a nod of thanks. "What little problem do you have today, Herr Maass?" He took a drink of his beer, and when he set it down, a few bubbles of foam clung to his moustache.

"I have a shipment . . . a medical shipment . . . which will require your special handling."

"A medical shipment? Isn't that a little out of your area?" Brandt asked. "I thought you were in the killing and maiming business, not the healing business." He laughed at what he thought was a joke.

"Yes, well, these particular items are quite sensitive," Otto replied without responding to Brandt's attempt at humor. "They are tracing agents."

"What are tracing agents?"

"It is a process whereby a radioactive element is introduced into the bloodstream, then tracked through the body by its nuclear signature. It aids doctors in their diagnoses."

"That seems like a rather ordinary shipment. Why would you need me?" Brandt asked.

"I'm afraid the level of radioactivity on this particular shipment is going to be quite high," Otto said pointedly.

"How high?" Brandt asked, taking another drink of his beer.

Otto took a deep breath. "Ten thousand deutsche marks high," he said.

Brandt was so startled by the amount that he jostled his glass, spilling some of his beer.

"Did you say ten thousand?" he asked in an awestruck voice.

"Yes. But it must go through without a hitch. I can't take the slightest chance that anyone would examine it after it is cleared."

"How is it being shipped?"

"In a hermetically sealed container, properly marked with all applicable radioactive symbols and accompanied by papers certifying it as a medical shipment within the limits of international nuclear regulations," Otto replied. "The weight is sixty kilograms."

"Destination?"

"Buenos Aires."

"Mein Gott, Herr Maass. You aren't shipping weapons-grade plutonium, are you?"

"I have told you all you need to know," Otto replied.

Brandt drummed his fingers on the table for a moment. "I will do it for fifteen thousand deutsche marks," he finally said.

"That is robbery. I have already offered you twice as much as I've ever paid before. I thought by doing so, we would avoid any unpleasant bickering."

"If you have offered twice as much, then it must be very important to you for this shipment to get through. And it cannot get through unless I allow it through. I think you will pay fifteen thousand."

"All right, I will pay fifteen thousand. But there must be no slipups. I want you to give it your personal attention," Otto said.

"I will take care of it," Brandt replied, smiling smugly over having successfully raised the price.

I got you, you arrogant little piece of shit, Otto thought. *I was ready to go to twenty thousand.*

EIGHT

Regency Hotel, Washington, D.C.

When Carter Phillips saw the maid leave Room 1215, he walked down to the end of the hall and picked up the house phone.

"Front desk."

"This is C. Phillips, room twelve-twelve. I'd like to be given room twelve-fifteen, please."

"Is there something wrong with your room, Mr. Phillips?"

"No, my room is fine, thank you. But I want twelve-fifteen in addition to this room."

"Very good, sir. I'll send the keys right up."

"Thank you."

Phillips returned to his room. After the keys arrived, he sat in the chair near the window and drank a Diet Coke as he enjoyed the view. The sun was just setting, and the slanting rays set fire to the Washington Monument so that it thrust into the air like a golden finger.

There was a knock on the door, and Phillips glanced at his watch. It was seven-fifteen. His visitor was exactly on time.

Picking up the keys from the table, he walked over to the door.

"Mr. Phillips, I'm Congressman Hugh Anderson. Thank you for agreeing to meet me." Anderson started into the room, but Phillips held up his hand and stepped out into the hall.

"We'll meet across the hall, in twelve-fifteen," he said.

"What? I don't understand."

"Let's just say it is a precaution," Phillips replied. "I've seen enough sting operations on *60 Minutes* and *20/20*. I don't care to have some hidden camera or microphone recording our conversation."

"I assure you, nothing like that is going to happen," Anderson sputtered.

"Then you won't mind changing rooms?"

Anderson sighed. "No, I don't mind at all. In fact, I appreciate your caution. I should have thought of it myself."

The two men stepped across the hall and into the other room.

"Now, what can I do for you, Mr. Anderson?" Phillips asked.

"First, let me tell you what I have done for you," Anderson replied. "This morning the House passed several routine housecleaning bills. On one of those bills, there was a rider which authorized the patent office to designate media-fusion as your personal patent, rather than grant it to Consolidated Technologies. That will prevent it from being seized during your upcoming bankruptcy hearings."

"Thank you," Phillips said. "With that patent, I can get on my feet again."

"As long as you have the funds to do so," Anderson said.

"Yes."

"I am about to provide you with a means of securing those funds. It is going to mean some risk for you, both economically and personally."

"Personally?" Phillips replied. "What do you mean, personally? What kind of personal risk is involved?"

"I won't lie to you, Mr. Phillips. A great deal of personal risk is involved."

"Be more specific, please."

"If things go wrong, you could be looking at long-term imprisonment," Anderson said. "But then, so could I."

"I'll take that risk."

"Under extreme conditions, it could be worse."

"What could be worse than long-term imprisonment?"

"You could be killed."

Phillips blinked a couple of times, then nodded. "And my economic risks?"

"You are going to have to come up with some seed money."

"How much money?"

"You will be contacted. The code word is Coldfire."

"Code word. You make this sound like I'm a Cold War spy or something. Double-oh-seven," he added with a weak laugh.

Anderson didn't laugh.

"Son of a bitch. It *is* something like that, isn't it? Are you asking me to spy against the United States?"

"There is no espionage involved," Anderson said. "But there is a need for a great degree of security. Now, are you in or out?"

"If I say no?"

"The bill I spoke of hasn't been signed yet. I introduced the rider. I can get it removed quite easily."

"No, don't do that. I need that patent."

"It's up to you."

Phillips got up and walked over to look through the window. It was getting dark now, and he looked down onto the lights of the city. He turned back toward Anderson.

"If I do this Coldfire thing, how much money can I make? I mean me personally."

"That is also up to you," Anderson said. "If you decide to go through with it, from the moment you are contacted until the deal is completed, you will be in charge. You will work out all the details, to include how much money you can make."

"I'm expected to work out the details?"

"Yes. Once I leave this hotel, Mr. Phillips, my part in this operation is over. I won't answer any questions, I won't offer any advice, I won't provide any assistance. And I would advise you not to try and involve me in any way. It's called building firewalls, and from here on, I would advise you to do the same thing."

"All right, I'm in," Phillips said.

Anderson stood up. "You'll be contacted."

"By who?"

"Good-bye, Mr. Phillips," Anderson said as he let himself out the door.

Phillips felt a queasy sensation in the pit of his stomach. Anderson didn't answer his last question, which meant the first firewall had just been erected. He suddenly realized that that also meant it was too late to back out.

He walked back over to look out at the night lights.

"Holy shit," he said quietly. "What the hell have I just gotten myself into?"

Airstrip outside Buenos Aires

The sound of frogs and nocturnal insects filled the air with the music of their incessant buzzing. Juan Punzi, a short, swarthy, middle-aged man, slapped against a mosquito as he leaned against the side of his ancient Chevrolet pickup truck. Glancing toward the bed of the truck, he saw that the tarpaulin had slipped to one side. He decided to reposition it, but before straightening the tarp, he pulled it back to examine his load.

What he saw was an aluminum container marked with radioactive symbols. The writing on the container was in Russian, German, and English. It read: MEDICAL SUPPLIES, RADIOACTIVE TRACER ELEMENTS.

While Juan was busy recovering the container, he heard the squelch break on the truck's two-way radio. A disembodied voice followed the break.

"Friendship, this is Medicare."

"Ernesto, they are here!" Juan called out into the darkness. He hurried to the front of the truck, reached in through the open window, and picked the microphone up from the seat. "Medicare, this is Friendship," he said, speaking into the mike.

Another man appeared from the darkness.

"Is that the Americans?" Ernesto asked.

"Yes."

"How much longer?"

"Soon. They won't speak again. They will signal with the microphone only, so we must get ready."

"That's good. I don't like being out here like this."

"Nor do I. But think of the money we are making," Juan suggested. "That will give you courage. Now, hurry, get the landing strip prepared."

Ernesto disappeared into the darkness while Juan stood by the open window of his truck. When he heard a series of squelch breaks, he flashed the truck's headlights three times.

The flashing of lights was not only a response to the squelch breaks, it was also Ernesto's signal. Out in the darkness, Ernesto threw a switch, which marked, but did not light, the runway with a long row of Christmas tree lights.

From the dark vault of the midnight sky came the sound of an approaching plane. Ernesto hurried back to the truck and stood beside Juan as they searched the night.

"There, I see him!" Ernesto said, pointing to a black shadow that passed across the blanket of stars. Within moments after Ernesto pointed him out, the approaching airplane's landing light came on, sending a long beam stabbing downward, illuminating hundreds of flying insects as it groped for the ground.

The business jet swooped down out of the sky, passing just over the top of the truck descending toward the end of the runway. There was a small chirp of tires as the wheels made contact with the macadam pavement, followed immediately by the roar of the thrust reversers. The landing roll took the plane to the far end of the runway before it turned around and started taxiing back. By now the landing light had been extinguished and as the plane approached, its outline could barely be made out by the red-and-green wingtip lights and the subdued red-orange glow coming from inside the cockpit.

As it reached this end of the runway, the right engine accelerated slightly, providing the plane with the dissimilar thrust required to turn it around and face back down the runway. Then the engines went to idle, and the cabin door opened. From the dimly lighted cabin, two men exited the airplane. Both were wearing pistol belts. They walked quickly to the truck, where one of the men pulled a thick brown envelope from his pocket and placed it on the hood. Juan opened the envelope and looked inside. In the ambient light he could see United States currency bound in two separate stacks by rubber bands. Each stack contained fifty one-hundred-dollar bills. Juan picked up one of the stacks and handed it to Ernesto. He began rifling through the other one.

"You plannin' on countin' it right here right now?" one of the men asked.

"I'm not counting, I am enjoying," Juan replied. He nodded toward the back of the truck. "There is the thing you have come for. Please take it. I am uncomfortable in its presence."

The man closest to the cargo picked it up, then made an abrupt move as if stumbling. "Boom!" he shouted.

"Que?" Juan gasped in quick fear, then realizing that the man was teasing, gave a sigh of relief.

The two Americans laughed.

"Very funny," Juan said. "Now, please leave quickly. I'm sure that word of your landing has already reached the local police. If they think you are drug-dealers, it could be bad for us."

"It might be worse for them," one of the men replied.

"What do you mean?"

The man nodded toward the plane, where a third person was standing in the doorway. Clearly visible was the submachine gun the man held, the butt of which rested on his hip.

"Please, leave quickly," Juan said. "I don't want any trouble."

"Don't be such a pussy. You're getting paid well enough for your end."

"We are getting paid to take chances, not to be fools," Juan said. "Please, leave before it is too late."

The two men carried the aluminum container back to the airplane, set it inside, then climbed in and pulled the door shut behind them. The door had barely closed when the engines were spooled up to full power.

Juan and Ernesto watched the airplane race back down the dark runway until it disappeared in the dark. A moment later the craft passed back over them, very low and going very fast. Then, just as it cleared the truck, the plane stood on its tail and shot nearly straight up. With both engines at full power, the roar was deafening.

For a moment, Juan and Ernesto were so caught up with the power and drama of the airplane taking off that they stood transfixed, watching the twin blue dots of the tailpipe until, finally, the blue exhaust flames became indistinguishable from the stars. By then the roar of the engines had become a distant, rolling thunder.

"What will they do with it?" Ernesto asked as the two men climbed into the truck.

"It is not our place to wonder what use they will make of it."

"Do you not think, even a little, of the consequences?"

"Ernesto, think not of the consequences. Think instead of the money we have earned this night. Five thousand dollars American for such a simple thing."

NINE

The boardroom of Consolidated Technologies Limited occupied almost half of the top floor of the Tanner-Dye Building. It was typical of many boardrooms across America, dominated as it was by a long elliptically shaped teakwood table, surrounded by a dozen red leather chairs.

Carter Phillips, CEO of Consolidated Technologies, stood at the window looking out at the bright sun jewels dancing on the surface of Lake Michigan. Two yawls, one with a red sail, the other with green, were running before the wind, though from here, their progress could be marked only by the wake they were leaving behind them.

As he stood at the window with his arms folded across his chest, Phillips could see, not only the lake, but also his own image reflecting back from the window. What he saw was a small man with watery blue eyes and thinning gray hair.

He looked old.

When did he get old? It seemed like only yesterday that his picture had graced the front cover of *News Events Magazine* over the heading AMERICA'S DOT-COM WUNDERKIND.

The article went on to explain how he had the Midas touch, how everything he touched turned to gold. It was on the basis of that reputation that he'd managed to sell investors on his business, Consolidated Technologies Limited.

In the beginning, CTL had great promise, and several bold gambles in the dot-com sector brought in over three billion dollars in the first eighteen months. Then the dot-com operations started going south and CTL slipped into serious financial difficulty. Now they were operating under a court-ordered restructuring plan designed, not to bring about a recovery, but merely to break up the company in a way that would provide all the creditors with as much return as possible on their accounts receivable. Once that was accomplished, CTL would close its doors.

For all intents and purposes, CTL was no longer a functioning company, for its marketing and services, as well as its research and development, departments were shut down. All that remained of a one-time workforce of fifteen hundred people were a handful of accountants. They were busy dissecting the corpse of what was once a viable business.

Phillips, who had invested and lost his own fortune in the company, was not listed as one of the creditors. The court had authorized payment to him of five thousand dollars per month so he could oversee the dissolution. As a result of his losses, he was faced with the prospect of selling his lakefront house in Kinelworth, his condo in Destin, Florida, and his Rolls Royce. He had already sold his yacht.

Then, when he'd had nowhere to turn, Congressman Hugh Anderson had made him a proposition. To be accurate, Anderson had not personally made the proposition.

What the congressman did was set Phillips up for the proposition that was to be made by arranging for the patent for media-fusion to remain the property of

Carter Phillips, rather than be regarded as an asset for Consolidated Technologies. Media-fusion was a method of using the electromagnetic field that surrounds any wire through which electricity is being conducted as a method of transmitting digital data.

Without that patent, Consolidated Technologies had no assets. With the patent, there was a possibility that Carter Phillips could make a comeback. All that remained was for Phillips to be prepared to do business with whoever approached him using the code word Coldfire.

Phillips didn't have to wait long. Less than twenty-four hours after his meeting with Congressman Anderson, Otto Maass, a German financier with whom he had done business in the past, had called him.

"I am very sorry to hear about your business difficulties," Maass said by way of opening the conversation.

"There are ups and downs," Phillips said without being too committal.

"I think perhaps you will be up again soon," Maass suggested.

"Yes, I certainly hope so."

"In fact, I have a proposal you might find interesting. I'm calling it Coldfire."

Phillips did a quick, short intake of breath, but said nothing.

"Are you there, Herr Phillips?"

"Yes, I'm here."

"You are aware of Coldfire, are you not?"

This was it. This was the contact Anderson had told him about. Phillips felt as if he were standing on the edge of an abyss. He had to back away, or take the leap, and the decision had to be made now. He took a deep breath.

"Yes, I know of Coldfire," he said resolutely.

"Good. Now, Herr Phillips, I am going to sell you

a product that you can then resell, at double your original investment. Your investment, to include the cost of handling, will be two and one half million dollars."

"Herr Maass, where am I going to get two and a half million?" Phillips asked. "Surely you realize that my company is in bankruptcy."

"Yes, I know," Maass replied. "But I am told by our mutual friend in Washington that until the final disposition has been made of all your debts, you have this much money available. You will only need the money for a short time, a matter of days."

"Then what?"

"Then you sell the product for five million, perhaps more."

"This must be some product if it will sell for five million dollars."

"It is," Maass said.

"You said the investment includes handling. What kind of handling?"

"It is, shall we say, a very sensitive product which will require transshipment through a third country. I would suggest Argentina. I have very good contacts there."

"What is the product?"

"You will find that out in due time."

"Wait a minute. You expect me to pay two and a half million dollars for something when I don't even know what I'm buying?"

"Yes, when the profit margin is this large."

"And I am to sell it for five million? How does one go about finding a customer who is willing to pay five million dollars for a product? Any product?"

"Finding a customer will not be difficult. Someone has already been contacted and is waiting for the product."

"Who is he? Where is he?"

"I cannot tell you his name."

"I don't understand, Herr Maass. If I don't know his name, how will I locate him?"

"The same way he will locate you," Maass replied. "By using the Internet."

Two and a half million dollars was a good sum of money. It wasn't large enough to save his failing business, but as this money would be tax-free—tax-free because he had no intention of claiming the income—it was certainly large enough to provide him with enough money to avoid personal bankruptcy. And at this point, he no longer cared what happened to the company, or to the workers the company had employed. He cared only about his own situation, and two and a half million dollars meant he could keep his house, condo, car, yacht, and most importantly, he thought with a smile, his mistress.

Soon after that conversation Phillips moved two and one half million dollars from the corporate account into a new account, which he called the Coldfire Account. He then paid one and a half million dollars to Otto Maass as purchase price for the product. Not until then did he learn what he had bought.

He almost backed out at that moment, but figured he was in too deep to pull out now. He had no choice but to go on. His next expenditure was to hire a pilot and a business jet to fly to Argentina to pick up his package. Realizing that he couldn't trust this delivery to any run-of-the-mill airfreight service, Phillips tapped some sources to find a mercenary pilot that would fly anywhere and do anything if the money was right.

The pilot was on that mission at this very moment, and if things had gone smoothly, he should be arriving from Argentina right about now. Unconsciously, Phillips glanced at his watch. He was so distracted that he had to concentrate hard on a simple thing like determining the time.

Hearing the door open behind him, Phillips turned to see Mr. Fitzgerald, one of the accountants who was taking the company apart. They were inventorying the stock right now. At one time CTL stock had sold for $126 per share. It stopped trading when it dropped below a quarter a share.

"Mr. Phillips?"

"Yes?"

"You have a telephone call, sir, from the Coldfire Corporation."

Phillips had told the pilot to use the word Coldfire when he wanted to talk to him.

"Thank you," Phillips said. Walking over to the conference table, he picked up the phone. Before he spoke, he looked directly at Fitzgerald, waiting pointedly for Fitzgerald to leave.

"I'll, uh, just be out here if you need me," Fitzgerald said awkwardly.

Phillips waited until the door closed behind Fitzgerald. "Did you get it?" he asked.

"Yes," the pilot answered.

"No problems?"

"No problems."

"Where is it now?"

"It's in the rental storage unit, just as we agreed."

"Very good. I will make a wire transfer of two hundred thousand dollars to your account today."

"Good for you," the pilot said. "Like our business motto says: 'If you've got the stash, call; then we will dash and haul.' "

Hanging up the phone even as the pilot was chortling over his own joke, Carter Phillips went over to the computer terminal, then posted the following

information on line at a Website called Gideon's
Sword.

PROJECT COLDFIRE
The Ultimate Solution
Bids Accepted

TEN

Ashen-faced, John Barrone got up from the chair, turned away from Simon Mason, then walked over to the window and looked down. Like most streets in Manhattan, Central Park West was dominated by yellow cabs, buses, and delivery trucks, though there were also a lot of private cars, many of them from out of state, the harried drivers trying to work their way through the slow-moving traffic.

He wondered how many people were within a one-thousand-yard radius of this exact point. Across the street a long line of children, holding hands two by two, were being led down into the park by two harried schoolteachers.

"A nuclear warhead stolen and smuggled out of Russia?"

"Yes," Simon said.

"What is the probability of accuracy on this?" John asked without turning away from the window. "I mean, how much credence do we give it?"

"My own sources tell me that the probability factor is very high, but both governments involved, Russia and Germany, have assured our State Department that there is nothing to it. And State feels that if we act as if there *is* something to it, it will strain our relations with them. State isn't prepared to do that."

"No, but evidently State is prepared to accept the consequences of a nuclear bomb being used somewhere in the U.S. if the report is true, I take it?"

"I believe it is called acceptable risk," Simon replied.

John snorted. "I wonder how acceptable the risk will be to the people who might have to come face-to-face with this thing."

"That's all factored into the equation."

John stroked his chin, then turned back to look through the window again. A man of average size and build, John kept himself in very good shape. He was in his early fifties, though considerably more agile than most of his contemporaries. His age showed most in his eyes. He had done a lot of living, and seen a lot of dying, in his fifty-three years.

Once again he turned away from the window to face Simon.

"You think General Grant is involved with this, don't you?"

"I honestly don't know," Simon replied. "I pray that he is not. He is exactly the kind of man who could make maximum use of a thing like this."

"I have to tell you, since our conversation a few weeks ago, I have looked into the situation with Grant."

"What have you found?"

"You're right, he does seem to have gone over the edge, at least in the extremism of his political views. But I have found no indication that he is involved in any real illegal activity."

"You worked with him once, didn't you?"

"Yes. During the Gulf War I did a black ops for him."

"You didn't mention that at our last meeting."

"No, I didn't."

"Do you like him?"

"He's a good soldier and one hell of a leader," John said. "I respect him for that."

"But do you like him?"

"He is a very mission-oriented soldier who doesn't let a little thing like extraneous death get in the way," John said, remembering the unnecessary killing of General Sin-Sargon's young aide, Lieutenant Kahli.

"Is the Arlington Lee Grant you know someone who would make use of a nuclear device if he had it?" Simon asked.

John ran his hand through his hair, then sighed. "Yes," he admitted. "If Grant thought the use of a nuclear weapon was necessary to complete his mission, he would use it."

"Do you remember, John, when you and your people were shadowing Task Force Clean Sweep and I asked, almost rhetorically, what the bad guys would surprise us with in the future?"

"I remember," John said.

"I guess it turns out that my question wasn't so rhetorical after all, was it?"

"I guess not," John agreed. He sighed. "I think it's time to assemble the team."

"I was hoping you would come to that conclusion. Look, John, I'm prepared to give you as much help as I can—that is, with the understanding that everything I tell you is deep-throat, so to speak."

"You'll be risking your career," John warned.

"I know, but anytime it comes to putting my country or my career at risk, I'll put my career at risk every time," Simon said.

"If the probability of a nuclear weapon winding up in rogue hands is as strong as you say it is, I don't know why none of the agencies have the balls to act on it, no matter whose toes they step on," John said.

"Come on, John, you remember how it is. The career agents have the balls, but not the authority. The political hack appointees have the authority, but not the balls."

"Yeah, I remember."

"I have to tell you, when I heard that you had left the Company and gone into business for yourself, I thought you were turning your back on all of us who stayed back to fight the good fight. I know now that you are still fighting the fight, only with a hell of a lot more flexibility. I found that out when you showed up unannounced in Wheeler County."

John chuckled. "Like I said, Simon. I was just passing through."

Bozier City, Louisiana

Don Yee was at the blackjack table in the Isle of Capri Casino in Bozier City, just across the river from Shreveport, Louisiana. A huge pile of chips were stacked in front of him, evidence that he was on a roll, and several of the casino patrons were gathered around to see just how far he could ride the streak.

A new dealer was summoned, and he arrived looking cool and crisp, in stark contrast to the sweating dealer he had just relieved. With a confident smile on his face, the new dealer broke the seal on a deck of cards and shuffled them smoothly and expertly, spreading the shiny new deck out on the green felt, then flipping them over in a waterfall effect.

"How are you doing tonight, sir?" the dealer asked. He looked at the pile of chips in front of Don. "Silly question, isn't it? You are doing great."

"Great, he's going to break the bank," one of the onlookers said.

"Oh, I hardly think it's as bad as all that," the

dealer responded. "The Isle of Capri has pretty deep pockets. You don't mind if I join the game, do you, sir?"

"No, I don't mind," Don answered. "So what have they done, called in their ace reliever to stop me?"

"Is that what you think I am?" the new dealer replied smoothly. "The ace reliever?"

"You've got that look about you."

"Ace reliever. Hmm, I like that. But I can't claim that. I'm just giving the other dealer a rest, that's all."

"Too bad. I would like the idea of going against the best."

The new dealer smiled confidently, almost arrogantly. "Oh, don't fret yourself, sir. I didn't say I wasn't the best."

The satellite phone in Don's pocket vibrated and he took it out to read the message on the screen. It said simply: "Meet."

Don began picking up his chips. The groans of disappointment from those who had gathered to watch, and the unctuous "No guts, sir?" from the dealer, didn't faze him as he walked away.

Beaumont, Texas

At the Holiday Inn Plaza on I-10 West, bomb-disposal specialists from all over the country had gathered for a conference designed to exchange information and learn the latest techniques. At the moment, they were seated in the Houston Room for dinner. Jennifer Barnes, who enjoyed the reputation of being one of the leading explosive experts in the nation, was seated at the head table. Shortly, she would be introduced as the keynote speaker. She was just beginning her tapioca pudding when her cell phone rang. She took the phone from her purse.

"Yes?"

"Meet," the voice said.

Jennifer hung up, then leaned over to the conference director. "You'll have to carry on without me,"
she said. "I must go."

The conference director watched in open-mouthed
disbelief as Jennifer got up from the table and left the
room, her tapioca pudding only half-eaten.

Paul Brewer was coaching a Little League football
game in Paducah, Kentucky. It was third and long in
the fourth quarter when the call came. He immediately turned the game over to his assistant coach and
left the field.

Linda Marsh was at the opera, sitting in the middle
of the row at a performance of *Madame Butterfly*, when
she got her message. She had to pass in front of half-
a-dozen men and women in order to excuse herself.
The men actually enjoyed it.

Chris Farmer was on a private shooting range in
Kansas City when he heard.

Lana Henry was in St. Louis, having dinner with a
wealthy stockbroker who thought, erroneously, that he
was about to score. The stockbroker had just excused
himself to go to the rest room, where he sprayed his
mouth a few times with a breath-freshener, prepara-
tory to "closing the deal" with her. The big smile on
his face disappeared when he returned to the table
and found Lana gone. She left a note scrawled, in
lipstick, on the table napkin.

"Sorry, had to run."

Mike Rojas was at a street festival in San Antonio.
He was wearing an oversized, fringed sombrero and
playing a tambourine when his pager called him.

Bob Garrett was having a Big Mac and fries at a
McDonald's in Cleveland when he was called.

* * *

Code Name Team Headquarters, somewhere in West Texas

The house sat in an isolated area, far enough from any major road that no one could just happen by. If a car was on the road, it was definitely coming to this house. It was a nice house, the kind of place to which a wealthy CEO might retire. It was stylish and spacious, without being outwardly ostentatious. A casual glance showed how cleverly the architecture managed to blend with the environment, making use as it did of stone and weathered wood. Even the tumbleweed that rolled by added to the intrinsic appeal of the house.

It was not until someone went inside that they could see how unique the house really was. In the room that might be a den in any other house, there was a dazzling array of electronic equipment. There were TV screens, computer terminals, faxes, and copiers. There was also a character-and-image-generator that could receive data from a dozen orbiting satellites, then project, onto a wall-sized screen, a detailed picture of just about any place in the world. Further, it could do all this in real time.

This was the headquarters of the Code Name Team, and when the Code Name Team's members arrived today, most would be seeing it for the first time, for this was the newest weapon in their large arsenal.

They began to arrive just before sunset. Jenny Barnes was first to arrive, driving up in a lusterless gray Humvee. Chris Farmer was next. He was driving a new Cadillac, and was closely followed by Mike Rojas, who was straddling a Harley. Lana Henry drove up in a nondescript rented Ford, and Paul Brewer turned heads when he showed up in a mint-condition 1957 Corvette, black, with red cove moldings.

When a small Robinson helicopter set down just in

front of the house, no one had to look twice to know that it was Don Yee.

Bob Garrett came in an '86 Dodge pickup truck, dented and faded red. The fine-tuned engine, however, belied the truck's pedestrian appearance. Linda Marsh rode up on a ten-speed bicycle, wearing a crash-helmet and a form-hugging spandex suit that showed off to perfection her athletically trim body.

"All right," Linda said, taking off her helmet and shaking free her long, black hair. "Who knows why we were called together?"

"Our fearless leader must know," Paul Brewer replied.

The only African American of the group, Paul had been an All-Star college football player, sure to go in the first round of the NFL draft. An injury sustained during the Orange Bowl game made the NFL teams shy away from him, so he wound up playing in the Canadian League. Although he had been out of professional football for ten years, his body-fat ratio was nearly the same now as it had been then.

"He hasn't arrived yet, has he?" Chris asked.

"Oh, he's here," Jenny answered. "He's the one who summoned us. You'll find him around back, barbecuing an elephant."

It wasn't really an elephant, though from the size of the piece of meat on the spit, it was easy to see how Jenny could make the comparison.

"Smells good," Don said, walking over to sniff the cooking meat.

"Roadkill would smell good to you," Jenny teased, referring to the small man's prodigious appetite. She didn't know what unique gene he possessed that would allow him to eat all the time without gaining an ounce. Whatever it was, she wished she could extract it, reproduce and bottle it, then sell it on the market. Such a product would make her richer than Bill Gates.

"What's up, Chief?" Paul asked as he pulled a little piece of the meat off the spitted haunch. "Why did you call us here?" He stuck the meat in his mouth, then smacked his lips appreciatively.

"Beer's in the cooler," John said. "Paper plates are over there. Get your food. You'll be filled in on everything as you eat. Don, did you do the computer research I asked you to do?"

"I did," Yee answered.

"Good. I'll be asking for some details later."

"Ladies and gentlemen, good evening," a new voice said as Wagner came out onto the patio from the back door of the house.

Although not a field operative, Wagner was very much a part of the team. He was the contact between the team and the consortium of wealthy financiers who backed them.

"Mr. Wagner will fill you in while you're eating," John said.

"Thank you, John," Wagner said. Clearing his throat, he looked out over the long picnic table at the group of men and women who were just beginning to eat their barbecue.

"Two weeks ago we received word from Baron Heinrich von Schenkle that a man named Otto Maass had come into the possession, through a black-market purchase, of a low-yield nuclear weapon."

"Von Schenkle? Isn't he one of the financiers who back our operation?" Paul asked.

"Yes," John said, answering for Wagner. Although everyone in the team had done enough investigating on their own to discover just who was behind them, Wagner felt honor-bound never to confirm or deny any of the information. John, on the other hand, believed that if the team members couldn't be trusted to know who was behind them, they couldn't be trusted for anything. Therefore, he had no compunctions about answering Paul's question.

"Who is Otto Maass?" Lana asked.

"Maass is one of Germany's most respected arms dealers," said Wagner. "He is very highly thought of by the German government."

"An arms dealer who is dealing in nuclear weapons? I didn't think nukes could be traded on the international market," Bob Garrett said.

"Well, they are not supposed to be."

"What does the German government say about it?"

"It seems that von Schinkle informed the German government of the fact that one of their citizens was now in possession of a nuclear weapon. But after no more than a perfunctory investigation, the German government concluded that there was nothing to the allegation. They suggested that von Schenkle may have been influenced by the fact that he and Maass are often competitors in business."

"Is it possible that the German government is correct?" Mike asked. "Could von Schenkle be improperly influenced by the heat of some previous competition?"

Wagner shook his head. "No, that is not at all possible. Von Schenkle is a man of great integrity. As you also know, he is a man of tremendous wealth, so he hired his own investigators to look into the matter."

"In that case, what does he need us for?" Chris asked.

"He doesn't need us," Wagner said. "We need us."

"What do you mean?"

John answered Chris's question. "It turns out that Maass bought the weapon from someone in Russia just as von Schinkle said. But, and this is what is frightening, Maass no longer has the weapon."

"Where is it?"

"This we do not know. But we fear that it may turn

up in the United States—that is, if it hasn't already done so."

"What?" several of the team asked at the same time.

"John, let me get this straight. Are you saying some of our own home-grown kooks, right here in the good old U.S. of A., may have gotten their hands on a nuclear bomb?" Jenny asked.

"I'm afraid so," John replied.

"Does the CIA confirm that?" Paul Brewer asked.

"Not officially," John answered. "Neither does the FBI, the National Security Agency, or any other federal agency."

"What do you mean, not officially?"

"I had a meeting with one of our friends in high places, Simon Mason. He is convinced of the accuracy of the report. However, for political purposes, our State Department has accepted the German and the Russian governments' assurances that there is absolutely nothing to the allegation."

"What makes Mason think there is anything to it?" Jenny asked.

"Because he learned, and we have verified, that the Russians have a nuclear device unaccounted for," John said. "I've already brought Don Yee into this operation because I wanted him to do some early computer sweeps for us. Don, you want to tell us what you found out?"

Don Yee swallowed his food, then washed it down with a swig of beer before he began to talk.

"In response to some parameters John gave me, I have been hacking into the Russian government's secret communications traffic. It turns out that about a month ago a man named Colonel Yuri Shaporin was quietly and summarily executed. Shaporin was commanding officer of a tactical-missile battalion in the Tamansky Division. His battalion has been demobilized and all their equipment turned it. When the equipment was inventoried, however, it turned out that Colonel Shaporin was short one five-kiloton warhead."

"Damn! Then it *is* possible that it made it over here," Paul said.

"Not only possible, highly probable," Wagner said.

"Lord help us," Linda said. "Can you imagine what some nutty group could do with an atomic bomb? How big is this thing anyway? What did you say it was? A five-kiloton warhead? It couldn't be that easy to smuggle something that big somewhere, could it?"

"Well, the Oklahoma City blast used a truck to smuggle the bomb, so size doesn't make that much difference if someone is determined to do it," John explained. "But to answer your question, a five-kiloton warhead isn't much bigger than one of the older-style video cameras."

Linda brightened. "Really? Well, if it's no bigger than that, how bad can it be?"

"I'll refer that to our resident explosives expert. Jenny, you want to answer Linda's question?" John asked.

"The yield of a five-kiloton warhead would be about one fourth the strength of the Hiroshima bomb, or twice as large as the Texas City explosion back in 1947. I mention Texas City because that was the largest non-nuclear, man-made blast ever. A five-kiloton warhead's absolute kill radius would be about a thousand yards from ground zero. In a densely packed environment, it could kill hundreds of thousands," Jenny explained.

John recalled his last meeting with Mason, and he thought again of the schoolchildren he had seen walking in the park. If the bomb were to go off in the hotel where he had stayed, the number of deaths would be staggering.

Several members of the team gave a low whistle.

"As you can see," Wagner said, "it is imperative

that we locate this bomb, then neutralize it and whoever has it."

"Any leads on where it might be?" Jenny asked. "I mean, does some extremist group here already have the bomb?"

"Right now, the prime suspect would be former General Arlington Lee Grant and his Freedom Nation group. But we don't think anyone has the bomb yet and if it is put on the market, there may well be free-for-all bidding to acquire it. Don, I asked you to run a check on all the militant Websites. What have you find out?"

Don chuckled. "I found out there are too damn many militant Websites to check them all. Some of them are maintained by fifth-grade computer whizzes, such as Government Sucks, Britney Spears Rules."

"Well, hell, what's wrong with that?" Chris asked, and the others laughed.

"On the other hand, I did find something interesting on a site called Gideon's Sword."

"Gideon's Sword?"

"It's a site that sometimes sells illegal weapons. You know, machine guns, rocket launchers, mortars, that sort of thing."

"Openly?" Paul asked.

"Yep. Right out there," Don replied.

"Why don't they shut it down?"

"There's no way it can be shut down. This is the Internet, remember? The World Wide Web? The U.S. Government can prevent a private citizen from owning such weapons, but they can't prevent them from being advertised for sale over the Internet. It has no control over what is put up on any of the sites."

"What did you find on Gideon's Sword?" Jenny asked.

"I printed it off," Don replied. He picked up a

piece of paper and read aloud. "Project Coldfire. The Ultimate Solution. Bids Accepted."

"Ultimate solution? That has a rather ominous ring to it, don't you think?" Lana asked. "A little like Hitler's Final Solution."

"I wonder what it all means," Chris Farmer said. "It's obviously an auction of some sort, but it mentions something called an ultimate solution and Project Coldfire. I wonder what that's all about."

"I would think the term Coldfire might give us a hint," John answered.

"How so?"

"Does the Manhattan Project mean anything to anyone?" John asked.

"Yes," Lana replied. "That was the operational name for the development of the atomic bomb."

"Correctamundo, wise lady," John said.

Lana beamed.

John continued. "During the Manhattan Project, *Goldfire* was the code word that was invoked anytime someone within the project needed the highest priority. It was said that a scientist who used the word 'Goldfire' would have precedence for anything he might need: equipment, manpower, location, transportation, or money. And he had this priority over anyone else in the government or military, from the President on down."

"So, you put those two together, Goldfire and ultimate solution—change one letter—and it doesn't sound good, does it?" Mike Rojas said.

"Well, here's something that makes it sound even worse," Don said. "I have seen the word Coldfire pop up in the correspondence of both Freedom Nation and Oppressed Brotherhood."

"Oppressed Brotherhood," Paul said. "The Oppressed Brotherhood is a militant black group. You mean they might be bidding for this against Freedom

Nation? Wow, you talk about your opposite ends of the spectrum."

"I think the possibility has to be considered that Freedom Nation and the Oppressed Brotherhood are not the only potential customers for Coldfire. No doubt it will be sold to the highest bidder."

"I can't imagine someone selling a nuclear bomb for peanuts," Mike said. "How would one of these groups come up with the money that would be required?"

"For something like this, there is every possibility that they could get some financial aid from foreign sources," John suggested.

"Like who?" Chris asked.

"Here is the real irony. The best potential for both these groups would be from the same foreign element. Because Freedom Nation has targeted Jews, they could very well receive aid from somewhere in the Middle East, maybe a rogue country like Iraq, or even a militant group. Hell, Hajji Aziz could finance this operation all by himself. And because so many African Americans have embraced the religion of Islam, Oppressed Brotherhood could tap into this same source of financing. It would be a win-win situation for the sponsors. All they would have to do is supply a little money, then sit back and watch Americans kill Americans."

"All right, let's say this nuclear weapon exists," Lana said. "And let's say that one of these groups manages to get their hands on it. What do they want it for? What do you think they will do with it?"

"Given that these two groups are at opposite ends of the spectrum, it could be that whichever group gets the weapon first will use it against the other group," Bob suggested.

"Well, then, hell, what do we care? Let the bastards

kill each other off," Paul said. "As far as I'm concerned, they'd be doing the world a big favor."

"True, and if they were out on an island somewhere, I would agree with you. But both groups are in the United States, which means there would be a lot of collateral damage and a lot of innocent people would be killed," John said.

"Okay, Chief, you're the head man here. What do we do now? Give us our marching orders," Don said. "Where do we go from here?"

"I don't want you to go anywhere," John said. "I want you right here, working with the computers. Hack into any system you think will give us information. If there is any piece of equipment you need . . ."

"Are you kidding?" Don interrupted. "If there is any piece of equipment I need, the chances are it hasn't yet been invented. I don't believe there is an information-gathering facility anywhere in the world superior to this one."

"Then you will be all right with staying here?"

Don rubbed his hands together. "More than all right. I'm going to love it," he said with eager anticipation.

"Bob, I want you and Chris to go to Dothan, Alabama. There is a white supremacy group there called the Wiregrass Chapter of the Alabama Knights of the White Orchid. There has been quite a bit of electronic communication between them and Freedom Nation.

"Mike, you do the same thing among the Latino gangs in Los Angeles."

"Whoa, you mean the homeboys are in on this thing?" Mike asked.

"I don't know if they are or not. But the Hispanic population is the fastest-growing segment of American society. So it would only be prudent to check them out."

"What about me?" Lana asked.

"I want you to stay here with Don. You'll be our liaison. Also, if any of us in the field need backup, I want everyone else ready to go at a moment's notice.

"Do I figure into this anywhere?" Linda Marsh asked.

"Yes, you do. You're going to go with Paul," John said. "As his woman. Sorry to put her off on you like this, Paul, but we all have a job to do," John said. He was obviously teasing, because Linda was a woman of exceptional, sultry beauty.

"I'll grit my teeth and bear it somehow," Paul said to the laughter of the others. "So, where are we going?"

"I want you to infiltrate the Oppressed Brotherhood."

"It's not going to be that easy," Paul said. "I might be black, but they are suspicious of everyone, and they'd off their own brother if they thought he was in with the pigs."

"Well, you'll just have to convince them that you are the kind of person they want," John said.

"There might be another problem," Linda suggested. "Blacks like those in the Oppressed Brotherhood are as racist as any redneck. They don't like to see a mixing of the races, so what are they going to say when they see Paul coming into their group with a white woman?"

John chuckled. "They aren't going to see him with a white woman."

"What do you mean?"

"Linda, you have black hair, brown eyes, and an olive complexion. You are every bit as dark as Lisa Bonet or Vanessa Williams."

"And every bit as beautiful," Paul added.

"If they can pass as black, you can pass as black," John concluded.

"There's one big difference," Linda said.

"What's that?"

"They aren't passing as black, they *are* black. Or at least, racially mixed."

"Sorry 'bout that, but you are as close as we can come," John said.

Linda was quiet.

"You have a problem with that, Linda?" John asked.

"Can we talk for a moment? I mean, privately?" Linda asked.

"All right. Suppose you and I take a walk."

While a pregnant silence fell over the others, Linda and John walked out into the yard. They were several feet away from the house before Linda spoke.

"Don't make me do this, John," she said. "Don't make me try to pass myself off as black."

"What the hell, Linda, are you that prejudiced?" John asked.

"No, it's not that. It's . . ." She paused for a moment before she continued. "All right, suppose I am prejudiced. It's no secret that a disproportionate amount of crime is committed by blacks. I just have no respect for them, that's all."

"You have no respect for blacks as a race? Or blacks as individuals? I mean, what about Paul? He is one of us."

"Paul is fine."

"I see. Paul is fine, but blacks in general aren't."

"You're putting words in my mouth. The point is, I do feel this way, and I don't see how I can keep that feeling from showing through if I try and pass as black."

"All right, Linda, if that's what you want, I'll send Paul in alone," John said. Turning, he started back toward the house.

"No, wait," Linda called out.

John stopped.

"I don't want Paul to go in without a partner."

"And I don't want you acting as his partner out of some feeling of guilt. You said it yourself, your prejudices might show through. If they do, you'll not only put yourself in danger, but you'll be jeopardizing Paul."

"I want to do it," Linda said.

John was unmoved for a moment; then he smiled. "All right, let's go back inside."

"What'll we tell Paul?"

"Tell him you're going to do it."

"I mean, about this, about our discussion?"

John laughed. "You think Paul doesn't know you're prejudiced? Hell, you wear it like a Rebel flag. But he's a pro. If you and he go in as partners, he'll be with you one hundred percent. Just as I know you'll be with him, one hundred percent."

When John and Linda returned to the house, all conversation stopped.

"Is everything all right?" Jenny asked.

"Everything is just fine," John said. "Right, Linda?"

"Right," Linda replied. Smiling, she walked over to Paul and rubbed her fingers lightly against his cheek. "Okay, baby, I'll be your woman," she purred. "And you know what they say, 'Once you've gone black, you don't go back.' "

The others laughed at Linda's antics. Then Jenny turned her attention to John. "What about me?" she asked.

"You're coming with me," John replied. "We're going to join Freedom Nation."

ELEVEN

Wiregrass, Alabama

A big WINSTON COUNTRY sign dominated the front of the little, weatherworn store. In small letters at the bottom of the sign were the words BELCHER'S GROCERY.

A rusty tin roof hung out over a board porch, though one side of the roof sagged badly. On the porch, two men sat in cane-back chairs, flanking an old, once-red cold-drink box. Both men were in jeans and T-shirts. One of the men was wearing an Auburn University hat; the other had a cap from the University of Alabama. A large spotted dog was sleeping in a curl next to the steps.

The store was on a blacktop road in an area known as the Wiregrass, about twenty miles southwest of Dothan, Alabama.

"Auburn and Alabama," Chris said as Bob parked his pickup truck in the dirt-and-cinder lot in front of the store. "What do you think the chances are that either one of them actually attended one of those schools?"

Bob chuckled. "If they had to wear caps from the last school they attended, it would probably be saying something like, 'Roberta Pearson Grammar School.'"

"Or the Alabama Reformatory," Chris added, and both men laughed.

The two men on the porch were drinking beer. The Auburn hat belched, then stood up and walked over to the edge of the porch. With absolutely no effort toward modesty, he unzipped his pants and began peeing over the side.

Bob and Chris got out of the truck and started toward the store. The dog was so secure in his position that he didn't even wake up when they stepped over him, onto the porch.

"I'm a-likin' your front tag," the man who was wearing the Alabama hat said, nodding toward the front of the pickup. The State of Alabama issues only a rear license plate; thus the front plate can be an expression of the driver's sentiment. Frequently these plates represent a favorite university or a state or Confederate flag. Bob was well aware of this, and had chosen the front plate on his truck accordingly. It was of a burning cross. A small Confederate flag fluttered from his radio antenna.

Looking at the man on the porch, Bob took a pouch of chewing tobacco from the front pocket of his bib overalls, grabbed some of the loose strings between his thumb and forefingers, then poked it into his mouth. He waited until he had worked up a chew before he responded.

"Do you now?" he asked, his reply almost a challenge.

"I do indeed," the Alabama hat said. "Hey, Frank, d'you see the front of his truck?"

Frank, the man with the Auburn hat, shook himself off, then turned back around even as he was zipping up his pants. "What's that tag mean, mister?" Frank asked.

Bob looked at the front tag on his truck, then back toward the two men.

"If you must know, it means that the cross of Jesus will save you from the burning fires of hell," he replied dryly.

Frank and the man with the Alabama hat looked at each other and smiled.

"You boys ain't from around here, are you?"

"We're from Foley, down in Baldwin County," Bob said.

"Foley, huh?" Alabama Hat asked. "You know a fella down there by the name of Emil Terrell?"

"Emil Terrell's my cousin."

"That a fact? Tell me, how's ole' Emil doin'?"

"Not all that well. He's takin' a vacation with the state right now. Serving five to ten for keepin' his mouth shut when the Feds come snoopin' around our . . ." Bob paused, spat a stream of tobacco juice over the side of the porch, then wiped his mouth with the back of his hand before he finished his answer. "Prayer meetin's."

Bob was able to answer that question because Don Yee had researched all the databases on known members of Southern white supremacist organizations, including the fact that Emil Terrell was currently serving time.

Alabama Hat smiled broadly. "Far as I'm concerned, Emil Terrell is a genuine hero. And if you his cousin, then by God, you all right with me."

Alabama Hat stuck out his hand. "The name's Arnie Stone," he said. "This here is Frank Norton."

Bob shook hands with Arnie, but just stared at Frank's proffered hand for a moment, then looked directly at him.

"If you don't mind, Frank, seein' as where I just seen that there hand, I reckon I'll pass on the handshake."

For a second Frank frowned, as if he had been offended, but Arnie laughed out loud. "He's got you there, Frank. Don't no one want to grab a'holt of a hand that's just been wrapped around that skanky-assed cock of yours."

"The name's Bob Jeeter," Bob Garrett said, introducing himself with the name he had chosen. He nodded toward Chris Farmer. "This big fella is Chris Neighbors."

"Chris Neighbors? Say, didn't you used to play football for Alabama?" Arnie asked.

"Mississippi State," Chris said. At six feet three-inches, 220 pounds, Chris actually had played football, but not for Mississippi State. He had been a tight end for Missouri, and not as Chris Neighbors, but as Chris Farmer.

"Yeah, yeah, I seen you play oncet. You was pretty good, but we beat you."

"No big thing," Chris replied. "When I was playin' for Mississippi State, ever'one was beatin' us."

Frank and Arnie laughed.

"You boys is all right," Arnie said. "You goin' be around a while? Or are you just passin' through?"

"We prob'ly goin' to hang around for a while. We're lookin' for some land to buy."

"They's some for sell up in Dale County."

"That's what we heard. I think maybe we'll go up there take a look," Bob said. "Listen, do you boys have any idea where we might find a chapter? I know how it is down in Baldwin County, when folks we don't know want to drop in to one of our, uh, *prayer* meetin's. You can't be none too careful. But if we goin' to spend any time up here, we'd sort'a like to be with our own kind."

Frank and Arnie shot a secretive look at each other, and for a moment, Bob thought he might have gone too far.

"I reckon you could attend one of our meetin's if you wanted to," Arnie said.

"You sure now? I know sometimes folks gets nervous, and we wouldn't want to be intrudin'," Bob said.

"Wouldn't be intrudin'," Frank said. "Hell, you boys is all right, I can tell that just by lookin' at you."

"It won't cause you no personal trouble? I mean, bringin' us in like this without gettin' permission from the Grand Google."

Frank laughed. "Tell 'em, Arnie," he said.

"Hell, boys," Arnie said proudly. "I am the Grand Google. If I say you boys can come to the meetin', you can come to the meetin'."

"That a fact?" Bob said. He stuck his hand out again. "It's a pleasure to meet you, sir. It's a pleasure and an honor."

Frank fished two beers from the ice chest, opened them, then handed them to Bob and Chris.

"Here, you boys look like you could use a beer," he said.

"Thanks."

Frank nodded toward the screen door. "You can pay Belcher. He's just inside."

East Los Angeles

Mike Rojas was a powerfully built, swarthy-complexioned man, approximately 180 pounds. Formerly with the Internal Security Division of IRS, he sometimes quipped that nobody had ever liked him anyway, so the IRS was as good a place as any for him to be. Mike was of Mexican descent and could speak Spanish, but his American roots stretched all the way back to Texas independence when his ancestor died inside the Alamo, one of the few Texas-born defenders to do so.

Despite his nearly two hundred years of American roots, he was the Code Name Team's entrée into any situation that required a Latino ethnic background. Because of that ethnicity, the Code Name Team sent him to Los Angeles to see if any of the Mexican gangs had anything to do with Project Coldfire.

When he pulled his '67 Impala to the curb in East Los Angeles's Pacoima Projects, he stopped near a building that was tagged with gang symbols and signs. An adjacent building sported a colorful mural of a vaquero on a prancing white horse. The stylized rider was dressed in black and wearing a silver-studded sombrero, while carrying the flag of Mexico.

The car Mike was driving was candy-apple red with a polish so deep that it looked as if someone could stick their arm elbow-deep into the paint job. The interior was rolled white leather, and the centerpiece was the steering wheel, made of chrome-plated, welded chain links. A perfect prism hung from the rearview mirror.

Mike popped the release, then got out and raised the hood. Leaning over, he began adjusting the carburetor. A low-rider Pontiac, black, with an impressive flame-job, slid to a stop beside him. Activating the hydraulics, the driver raised, then lowered the car on its wheels.

"Homeboy," the driver said. "You got problems?"

"Nothing I can't handle," Mike answered.

The Pontiac pulled to the curb in front of Mike; then four young men got out. All four were showing colors, wearing orange and black starter jackets. Their shoes had orange and black laces, and one of them was wearing a glove on his right hand. The one with the glove spread his legs and stared at Mike.

"We're the Chicano Royals," he said.

"Is that a fact?" Mike replied, his voice showing his lack of interest.

"You're on our turf."

"I'm just passin' through."

"No, you don't understand. You don't just pass through someone else's turf," the one with the glove said. He walked up to the Impala and rubbed his bare hand across the smooth paint job.

"You got to get permission from the Chicano Royals. Comprende?"

"No chinga con mí," Mike said with a growl.

"Don't fuck with you? Is that what you said?"

"That's what I said, man. Don't touch the car," Mike said. "Fingerprints ruin the paint."

"What's your name, man?" the driver of the Pontiac asked. From his swagger, and the fact that he was driving, Mike realized that he was the leader of the little group.

"Cisco Kid," Mike replied.

"Cisco Kid?" the driver replied, confused for a moment. Then he laughed. "Ah, yes, the Cisco Kid. Very funny." He touched the car again. "Nice wheels."

Mike brushed his hand away. "I told you, don't touch the car."

Almost faster than the eye, the driver of the Pontiac had a switchblade knife in his hand. Crouching, he stuck the knife out, the point of it weaving little circles in the charged air that separated them.

"Man, you don' be worryin' do I touch your car. What you got to worry about is me and this knife. I'm goin' to fillet you, like openin' up a fish."

"Cut 'im, Ernesto. Cut 'im," one of the others said.

Ernesto held his left hand out, palm up, curling his fingers forward in invitation.

"Come on, homeboy," Ernesto said. "Come on. Let me see what you got."

"What I've got," Mike said, reaching into his back pocket, then pulling out a pistol, "is a .44 Magnum." Going into a crouch as if on the target range, and holding the pistol in both hands, he pointed it at Ernesto's head. "Step to one side," he said menacingly. "I don't want to have to clean your brains off my car."

For a moment, Ernesto looked frightened. Then a nervous smile spread across his face. He had been using his bare hand as an invitation for Mike to come ahead. Now he turned that same hand palm out, as if signaling him to stop.

"Wait a minute, wait a minute, amigo," Ernesto said. "I was just teasing." Ernesto folded the knife shut and put it away. Not until then did Mike lower his pistol.

"Nice colors," Mike said, nodding toward the orange and black jackets all four were wearing.

That night, Mike emptied his Chinese takeout meal on a table in the motel room, then switched on the evening news. He was just reaching for his sweet and sour pork when a flash of light lit up the room. A second later he heard the roar of an explosion. Hurrying to the window, he looked out into the parking lot and saw his car on fire.

"Amigo!" someone shouted from outside. "Amigo, where are you? Which room are you in, amigo?"

Mike saw the flame-job Pontiac and the four homeboys he had encountered earlier in the day.

"I know you wanted a flame-job, man! I saw you lookin' at my flame-job, man, so I give you one, too! Where are you, amigo? What is your room number? Come out and we can talk!"

All up and down the motel, doors to the rooms were opening as residents looked outside to see what was going on. As they did, the homeboys started shooting, indiscriminately spraying bullets toward the motel. Windows crashed and women screamed. The homeboys laughed out loud.

"We know you are in there somewhere, amigo!"

one of them shouted. He fired again, and Mike heard another window shattering.

Mike stepped outside.

"There he is, man!" someone shouted, and all four of them started shooting. Mike ran toward the corner, where the two sections of the motel were divided by a passageway. Bullets whined by his ears and hit the ground around him as he ran.

"Get him, man! Don't let him get away!"

Darting around the corner and into the passageway, Mike saw a high board fence at the rear. A Dumpster sat just in front of the fence. Running toward the Dumpster, he climbed onto it; then from the top of the Dumpster, he climbed to the top of the fence. From there, it was fairly easy to pull himself up onto the roof.

"Where'd he go?"

"He went into there, man, between the two buildings. Go see if he's in there!"

"I'm not goin' in there by myself, man. You crazy?"

Once Mike was on top of the roof, he bent forward in a crouch, then ran back to the front edge of the roof. Looking down on the parking lot, he could see the four homeboys crossing the open area, their pistols in their hands. Most of the residents had retreated back into their rooms by now. Their doors were closed and all the lights were out. As a result, the motel was dark, except for the little green neon tubes that outlined the building.

"Ricardo. You see him, man?"

Mike stood up on top of the roof, but was unseen by any of the four gunmen. From there he had a clear shot at all four of them, and had he wanted to, he could have picked them all off.

"No, man, I don' see nobody," Ricardo replied.

"You assholes looking for me?" Mike called down to them. He started firing at them, intentionally missing, but coming close enough that they could feel the hot breath of the bullets as they sped by.

"Holy shit, man, he's on the roof!" one of them yelled.

The four started running toward back toward the Pontiac. They returned fire, but it wasn't aimed fire; they were doing nothing more than holding their pistols up and shooting back over their shoulders.

Mike shot out the car windows, then put a few holes in the doors and the hood just so they wouldn't get away without any damage. He watched as they peeled out of the parking lot, laughing when the hood flew up. It ripped off, then rolled across the top of the speeding car, landing in a shower of sparks in the street behind them.

By now Mike could hear the sound of approaching sirens, and he knew that either one of the residents or the manager had called the police. Quickly, he scrambled down to the ground, then ran along the back side of the motel until he came to his room. Forcing open the bathroom window, he crawled back inside, and was sitting up in his bed watching TV when the police knocked on his door.

"So, finally you come," he said as he opened the door. "Man, there was a lot of shooting here." Although Mike had no Latino accent, to hear him speak now, one might think he had just come up from Mexico last week.

"We got here as quickly as we could," the police officer responded. "Can you shed any light on what was going on here?"

"No, man, I don' know anything. I heard the noise, but I was too scared to look outside, man."

"That was probably the smartest thing for you to do," the policeman replied. He pointed to the Impala, which was no longer burning, but was now a smoking, blackened hulk. "Do you know who owns that car?"

"No," Mike said, "but I bet whoever owns it must be very mad now."

Mike was able to lie confidently because he knew there was no way the car could be traced to him.

"Yeah, you'd think whoever owned it would be upset enough to be out here right now, trying to find out who did this, wouldn't you?" the policeman asked. "Unless he knows more than he is willing to share with us."

"Like what?"

"Some of the witnesses say they saw a gun battle between one of the residents and the four men who drove off. I believe the resident who was returning fire was the owner of that car."

"Did you check the motel register?" Mike asked. "Maybe you will find some clue there."

"Nothing there," the policeman said. He looked back toward the parking lot. By now it was filled with other policemen and curious residents. "Which car is yours?"

"Car? I don' have no car, man. I come here by bus," Mike replied. "I was just watching television when all the shooting started. I got very scared, so I got under the bed. Do you think it will be safe to spend the rest of the night here?"

"They're gone now, I don't think they'll be back. You can go back to bed. On top of it this time," the policeman added with a little laugh.

"*Gracias*, man," Mike said. "It's good you are here. I feel more safe now."

"Well, that's what we get paid for," the policeman said. "You just stay inside and you'll be all right."

After the policeman left, Mike picked up his chopsticks, and was just getting back into his sweet and sour pork when the phone rang.

"Yes?"

"This is Don," Don Yee said. "Find anything on

Yellowspark?" Yellowspark was the agreed upon code to inquire about Coldfire.

"Nada."

"That's cool."

Mike terminated the conversation then. Everything that was necessary had been said. There was no need to mention the incident that had just happened. For one thing, there was the possibility that the police now had the phones tapped. And for another, whatever had just happened had nothing to do with why he was here, and to mention it to Don Yee now would just complicate things.

Detroit

Paul Brewer parked the cherry 1957 Corvette, black, with red cove moldings, at the curb near a small barbecue stand. Walking around the car, he opened the door for Linda, then escorted her to one of the three picnic tables that sat outside the stand.

"You wait here, baby," Paul told her.

Paul walked up to the customer window and ordered two barbecue sandwiches. While he was waiting for the sandwiches, he turned toward a nearby table where he saw three black men. One of the men was openly leering at Linda, and when Paul glanced back toward her, he saw that she had leaned forward across the table in such a way as to allow her breasts to nearly spill out of the boat-neck shirt she was wearing. It was a provocative pose, designed to have the exact effect it was having.

"What the fuck you lookin' at?" Paul asked angrily.

"You think you King Shit, don't you?" the one who was leering at Linda asked. "Got yourself a fine car and white woman. You one sportin' nigger, ain't you?"

The others laughed. All three of the men were wearing dark glasses. The one who was talking was also wearing a lot of gold chain.

"She ain't white."

"What you talkin' about? Don't tell me she ain't white. She's as fuckin' white as the Queen of England."

Paul looked back at Linda and smiled. "She ain't white, she's shine. She's fine shine, and she's all mine. Just like the car."

"All yours, huh? The way she showin' her tits, looks like she's anyone's who wants her. You think you goin' to be able to hang onto her?" the gold-draped one asked.

Paul turned toward the heckler, squared his shoulders, and let his arms hang loose but ready by his side. "Now, let me ask you this, muthafucker," he said menacingly. "You think you the one can take her from me?"

A former All-Star college and all-Canadian League football player, Paul was a very imposing figure. If the gold-chained one thought he could intimidate Paul because he had a couple of his friends with him, he began to have second thoughts when he saw Paul bristle.

"Hey, take it easy, man. I ain't after your woman," he said. "I'm just tryin' to make friendly conversation, that's all."

"Don't be friendly," Paul said. "I ain't in no fuckin' mood to be friendly."

"Here your sandwiches," the old, gray-haired operator of the barbecue stand said, passing the two sandwiches through the window.

Paul took the sandwiches, then returned to the table and handed one of them to Linda.

"Are you trying to get me killed?" he asked under his breath.

"You said you wanted to get noticed," Linda replied quietly. She smiled broadly. "I was just doing my part."

"Uh-huh," Paul said as he took a bite of his pork sandwich.

"Go with me on this," Linda said under her breath. Then, much louder, she said, "Baby, you got to take it easy. You got a big chip on your shoulder. The man was just lookin', that's all. Don't you want me lookin' nice for you?"

"Lookin' nice for me, yeah," Paul said. "But you don't have to give an eyeful to ever' man you see."

"You need to calm down some. Don't go tryin' to get into the face of ever'one you meet."

"Yeah? Well, I don't like anyone fuckin' with me," Paul replied.

"Like that cop down in Memphis? Is that what he was doin'? Was he fucking with you?"

There was no cop in Memphis, and Paul and Linda hadn't worked out any sort of script between them, but he stayed with her, just to see where she was taking them with this line of conversation.

"Only reason we got stopped is 'cause we're black."

"That's just the way things are, baby. You know that. And you shouldn'a hit him so hard. "Now the man is really going to be comin' down on you."

"I told you, don't be worryin' about it," Paul said. "You know how dumb those cracker muthafuckers are. They prob'ly still lookin' for me back in Memphis."

"Still, that was a foolish thing, taking on three of them like that."

"Lily-white maggots," Paul said. "Wasn't much to it. All I had to do was growl at them and two of 'em shit in their pants."

Linda laughed. "You did have them scared of you."

"White sons of bitches, they think they control everything."

"They do, baby. They do," Linda said.

"Yeah, well, one day it'll be different."

"You always sayin' that. Ain't nothin' goin' to change. Ain't nothin' ever goin' to change. It's a white man's world. You just got to get used to it, that's all."

"No, I don't got to get used to it," Paul said. "All I got to do is change it."

Linda laughed. "Big man, you're goin' to change the world."

"That's right, baby. I'm goin' to change the world."

Without being obvious, Paul glanced over at the table near him to see how the little performance he and Linda were putting on was being taken. From the look of interest on all the men's faces, it was playing well.

They weren't in Detroit by accident. Detroit was the home of the Oppressed Brotherhood, a militant black gang with the avowed purpose of "overthrowing Whitey, and establishing a new Black Order." They even had their own Website, a resource that Don Yee had made good use of.

"Hey, you," one of the men at the nearby table called.

Paul glared at him. "You still tryin' to get in my face, man? I thought we had this all settled."

"Hold it, hold it, I ain't tryin' to get in your face. I'm just tryin' to make friends, that's all. My name is Ibo Mogombi."

"Ibo Mogombi? You born with a name like that?"

Ibo smiled broadly, causing his gold tooth to flash in the afternoon sun. "I named myself that," he said. "What's your name?"

"Paul Clark."

"That ain't your name. That's a tag that was hung on you by Whitey."

"Whitey ain't never hung nothin' on me."

"Uh-huh. And ain't no whitey cop ever stopped you just 'cause you're black either, is there?"

"When you going to stay the fuck outta my business?"

"Look, you want me to walk away, I will," Ibo said. "But I heard you and your woman talking. You the kind of person we're lookin' for."

"What do you mean, 'we're lookin' for'? Who is we?"

"The Oppressed Brotherhood."

"Never fuckin' heard of it."

"You will," Ibo said. "The whole world is goin' to hear about us."

"Is that a fact?"

"Yeah," Ibo said. "You see, you talkin' about changin' the world, but you ain't doin' nothin' about it."

"I might not change the world," Paul said. "But by God, Whitey is goin' to know I was here."

"You can do more than let Whitey know you're here," Ibo said. "If you throw in with us."

"The Oppressed Brotherhood?"

"Yeah."

"Throw in with you to do what?"

Ibo smiled, flashing his gold tooth again. "Why, to change the world, man."

TWELVE

Fort Freedom, Missouri

A powerful mine exploding just in front and slightly to the left of Jennifer Barnes caused her ears to ring and flashed its heat against her face. Mud, water, tiny shards of gravel, and burning bits of gun-cotton rained down on her as smoke from the blast drifted off through the gray, rain-washed air. Just inches above the advancing platoon, machine-gun bullets cracked loudly in their deadly transit.

Jenny looked at the others around her. They were wriggling on their bellies through explosive charges, maneuvering across a machine-gun-raked muddy field, sliding under concertina wire, rolling over logs, and trying to maintain their weapons in firing condition while keeping themselves below the kill zone. When she looked toward the far side of the field, she could see the four machine guns at the objective. Terrifyingly, she could also see the winking glow of tracer rounds flashing just overhead.

"Only twenty more meters," Jenny gasped, measuring the distance between herself and the objective. "Please, God, only twenty more meters! Let me live through this!"

She flinched at another explosion. The concussion of this one was great enough to knock her helmet off. Quickly, she scooped it up and put it back on, barely cognizant of the liquid mud, which oozed down over her ears, matting her hair and sliding under her shirt. She was totally covered with the stuff.

Taking a deep breath, she made several more desperate snakelike lunges forward, then clambered over the last berm.

She was there! She made it!

"Up here, up here!" someone was shouting. Checking the machine guns, Jenny saw that her last rush forward had carried her far enough beyond them to take her out of their field of fire. Instead, the bullets were whipping across those few unfortunate souls who were still mired in the mud of the open field. Wearily and with shaking knees, she stood up and, holding her rifle at high port, ran as fast as she could run at a crouch toward the point at which they were to rendezvous. Reaching her goal, she belly flopped down onto the wet grass, where she lay gasping for air, painfully aware of every heartbeat as it drummed inside her chest. Behind her, the machine guns maintained their firing, and the explosions continued.

"Cease fire, cease fire!" a voice shouted over the loudspeaker.

Abruptly, the guns stilled.

For a long, breathless moment, there was dead quiet . . . an unearthly quiet when contrasted to the din of just a few seconds earlier. In the distance Jenny could hear a train, its peaceful, everyday sound incongruous with her surroundings.

"Congratulations! You have just successfully completed the toughest and most realistic infiltration course in the entire United States!" the instructor said.

Cheers erupted. Jenny got up, then watched a dozen other mud-caked apparitions rise from the earth, giving each other high fives while wide, happy smiles spread across olive-drab-and-black-camouflage-painted faces.

Jenny saw John Barrone standing under a tree on top of a small rise, his arms folded across his chest, watching the proceedings. Though John was wet from the rain, he wasn't soaked, as the tree was providing him with some shelter. Moreover, he wasn't covered with mud, because he had not gone through the infiltration course.

John chuckled as Jenny came up to him. "You look like a mud ball."

Jenny pulled her mud-caked clothes away from her body. "I've got mud in places where I didn't even know I had places," she said. She filled her hand with mud, then playfully pressed it against John's cheek.

"Hey, if I wanted to get muddy, I would have accepted General Grant's invitation to go through the infiltration course."

"I can't believe you didn't."

"I can't believe you did."

"I figured one of us should do it, just to show we are serious about joining up with these people."

John and Jenny were in the Ozark Mountains of South Central Missouri, at a place called Fort Freedom. Fort Freedom, the headquarters of Freedom Nation, was a full-fledged military camp, complete with rifle ranges, infiltration courses, confidence courses, and a three-thousand-acre bivouac area.

They had arrived on the scene two days earlier, turning off Highway 60 onto a small, private dirt road. The road was blocked off, and a skull-and-crossbones sign issued a very specific warning against unwanted intruders.

WARNING
Private Road
You are entering the independent territory of
FREEDOM NATION
Borders guarded by armed sentries
Enter at your own risk

Disregarding the sign, John had opened the gate, then started up the small dirt road. The road narrowed until there was barely room for the Jeep as it followed a torturous path along a cut through the hills. As the way became even more difficult, John had to slip the Jeep into four-wheel-drive to maintain forward progress.

Suddenly there was a loud sound of breaking limbs and creaking rope as, abruptly and unexpectedly, a deadweight log swung down in front of them. John slammed on the brakes, managing to stop just short of a large, spike-studded log. Had the pendulum motion of the log not been arrested by the ropes from which it was suspended, it would have crashed into the Jeep.

"What the hell?" Jenny asked.

John put the Jeep into reverse, but before he could back up they heard the cracking sounds again as a second log, as large and as spiked as the first, fell to the road behind them. They were now effectively trapped. Three men, wearing camouflage clothing and with their faces painted in shades of forest-green and mud-brown, appeared out of the woods alongside the road. All three were carrying assault rifles.

"Hold it right there, mister!" one of the uniformed men called out. He and the two men with him raised their rifles to their shoulders, aiming at John and Jenny.

John looked at the logs in front and behind the Jeep, then shrugged.

"Doesn't look like I have much choice but to hold it," he said.

"What are you doing here?"

"We've come to join up," John said.

"Join what? Mister, we ain't doin' nothin' but huntin' deer in here."

John looked at the shoulder patches the men were

wearing. The patches showed the silhouetted faces of a man and woman. Crossed rifles were behind the faces. The words "Freedom Nation" arched across the top of the patch.

"I'm sure General Grant wouldn't mind having a couple more people join—" John paused before he added pointedly—"the hunt."

"General Grant? I don't know any General Grant. Who are you talking about?"

John pointed to the shoulder patches the three men were wearing. "I'm talking about Arlington Lee Grant, the head of Freedom Nation," John replied. "And if you three aren't members of Freedom Nation, then you are desecrating the honor of a lot of good men and women by wearing those shoulder patches."

"What'll we do, Cletus? He knows who we are," one of the three men asked the leader.

"Shut up," the leader replied. Cletus rubbed a finger alongside his nose for a moment, then took the radio from his utility belt and held it to his lips.

"This is Watchdog. We have a man and woman on the road in the containment area."

"Who are they?" a metallic voice replied.

Cletus looked questioningly at John and Jenny. "You heard the man," he said. "What's your names?"

"My name is John Barrone. "This is Jenny."

"Jenny what?"

"Jenny is enough," John said. "I'll vouch for her."

Cletus snorted what might have been a laugh. *"You'll* vouch for her? Mister, you talk like a man with a paper asshole. You don't even have anyone to vouch for *you*. How are you going to vouch for *her*?"

"Give your friend my name," John said, nodding toward the radio. "Have him check with the general."

Cletus spoke into the radio again. "He says his name is John Barrone. He wants you to mention his name to the general."

"Wait," the voice over the radio responded.

Cletus lowered the radio. "They're runnin' a check on you," he said.

"Good. I would be disappointed if they didn't."

"In the meantime, maybe I can save them a little time by asking you a few questions of my own," Cletus suggested. "You up to a little test?"

"Try me."

"What are the Eighty-eight Precepts?"

"They are the natural laws that govern our lives, as laid down by David Lane, a hero of the white race."

"What is The Promise?" Cletus asked.

"The Promise, as stated by the martyr Luke Clendenning, states: 'When the day comes, we will not ask whether you swung to the right or whether you swung to the left; we will simply swing you by your neck,' " John said.

"Yeah, and good enough for the bastards," Cletus replied, laughing.

The radio voice popped on. "The general says ask him what was the name of General Sin-Sargon's aide."

"What?" Cletus asked.

"Never mind," John said. "I caught the question. The aide's name the general is looking for is Lieutenant Kahli."

Cletus repeated the name in the radio.

"Yeah, that's it. Let 'em in."

That was yesterday. Last night they had stayed as General Grant's "guests" in one of the small cabins. They were told they were guests, though John had the distinct impression that if they had tried to leave last night, they would've been stopped.

It was during a philosophical discussion with General Grant that John and Jenny were invited to participate in a training exercise.

"We are running the infiltration course this afternoon, and I'd love to have you join us," he explained. "We'll be advancing across no-man's-land, raked with machine-gun fire, and forced to maneuver through a network of high explosives. I believe we have the most thorough infiltration course in the military world, and I would be interested in your opinion."

"I'd be happy to participate, General," Jenny said.

John, on the other hand, turned down the general's offer, and now found himself standing with a mud-caked Jenny on a small hill at the end of the infiltration course.

"Hey, I'm proud of you," John said. "You managed to keep your ass down for the entire time."

"In case you didn't realize it, there were bullets just a few inches over my head," Jenny said. "It was either keep my ass down, or get a bullet in the tush."

"I see what you mean," John replied.

"Attenhut!" someone shouted, and all who had just completed the infiltration course came to attention as General Grant walked over to join them.

"At ease, at ease," General Grant said. He smiled at them. "Congratulations, all of you. You are as fine a group of soldiers as I have ever commanded."

Arlington Lee Grant wasn't just making small talk. A graduate of West Point, he had served as a helicopter pilot during the Vietnam War, winning the Distinguished Flying Cross. By the time the Gulf War came around he was a lieutenant colonel. That was when John had met him for the first time. Grant's last assignment, before he got into difficulty with the military, was as an Army brigade commander, a brigadier general on the road, some said, to becoming the Army's Chief of Staff.

"Being named after two of our nation's most famous generals, Lee and Grant, wasn't enough for him," people used to say of General Grant. "He's also named Arlington. That takes in all the heroes who are buried in the National Cemetery at Arlington, Virginia."

"And you, young lady, did exceptionally well," General Grant now said to Jenny. "I kept my eye on you."

"You kept your eye on me? I'm impressed," Jenny said.

"Hah," John said. "What's so impressive about that? You are a beautiful woman. It's easy for a man to keep his eyes on you."

General Grant laughed. "Right you are, John, right you are. I take it you two will be in Liberty Hall this evening for my talk?"

"I wouldn't miss it for the world," Jenny said.

"Good, good. I've had Sergeant Major Clay select quarters for you. I'm sure you remember Sergeant Major Clay, John. He was part of our little soiree in Iraq on the evening before hostilities broke out."

"I remember him well," John said. "I didn't know he was with you. I haven't seen him since we arrived."

"He was running some errands for me," Grant said. "He just returned to garrison this afternoon. I hope you don't mind that they are separate quarters, but you aren't married and we are very strict about the morals of our people. I believe it is the lack of a moral code, as exemplified by one of our recent Presidents, that has caused the country to fall into its present condition."

"General, I had a laptop in my Jeep," John said. "I wonder if I might have it returned to me?"

"Certainly," General Grant replied. "As soon as Mr. Coker inspects it."

"Inspects it?"

"I'm sure you understand the need for absolute security. Our enemies are all about us. Felix Coker is our resident computer expert. Once he ascertains that there is nothing on your computer that could do harm to us, it will be returned to you. With the caveat that it be subject to unannounced inspection at any time."

"All right," John agreed. "I have nothing to hide. And I do appreciate the need for security and respect your diligence."

Code Name Team Headquarters, West Texas

Don Yee was just putting pickles on his ham, cheese, bacon, lettuce, tomato, and avocado sandwich when he heard a dinging sound coming from the computer. The dinging sound meant that an Internet inquiry was being made about John Barrone. Taking the sandwich with him, he hurried over to his station and watched the monitor.

Don had created several Internet entries for John Barrone. He had also tapped into all the Internet search engines so that any time an inquiry was made about John, he would be notified.

Don took a bite of his sandwich as he watched Yahoo fill the screen with possible sites in response to the inquiry. The inquirer chose a Web page that was entitled Aryan Victory.

That was one of the pages Don Yee had created, borrowing liberally from several militia and white power pages that were already in existence. Seeing that the inquirer had chosen his page, Don smiled broadly.

"Got you," he said as he took another bite of his sandwich and became a silent and unseen witness of the mysterious Web surfer.

Fort Freedom, Missouri

Felix Coker, Freedom Nation's resident Web surfer, watched the screen as matching sites for the information he had sought on Google.com began to come up on the screen. He chose Aryan Victory, then waited for the download. When the download was complete, he slid his glasses up his nose, then leaned forward to read the copy.

> *The Shield was formed by Lucas Jay Clendenning and his wife, Emma. Clendenning's aim was to quit talking and start acting towards a White American Bastion in the Pacific Northwest, and ultimately total Aryan victory. After decades of all "go" and no "show," Clendenning and his brave men put their lives on the line to secure the existence of our people and a future for White children.*
>
> *In its first year, the Shield began accumulating a war chest for its real-life revolution when they liberated $369 from a Memphis porno shop. Soon thereafter, a counterfeiting operation was launched at the Aryan Nations compound in Northwest Arkansas, but was exposed and set back when Shield member Billy Carroll was arrested for passing a counterfeit $50 bill. Carroll was eventually convicted, but jumped bond and went underground. Clendenning moved his operation to Oklahoma. Shortly thereafter, Luke Clendenning's cause was helped immeasureably by John Barrone. John Barrone, a CIA agent who grew frustrated with the interference of the Zionist Occupied Government, single-handedly liberated $125,000 from a bank in Little Rock. Using the money thus acquired, Barrone bought his way into The Shield.*
>
> *This reallocation of enemy resources into the hands of The Shield escalated the following year when a Shield member diverted police by exploding a bomb in an Oklahoma City theater, while John Barrone liberated an armored car parked outside a department store, this time seizing $500,000.*
>
> *Spurred on by the success of the first armored car robbery, Luke Clendenning and John Barrone planned*

a second armored truck robbery near Houston. This holdup yielded the group $3.8 million. The money from this, the largest armored car heist in history, was used in part for vehicles, equipment, and weapons. At about this time, a Jewish center was bombed in Dallas, resulting in the death of several Jews. Luke Clendenning felt it was necessary for The Shield to relocate, so he purchased a large parcel of land in Oregon which he intended to use for guerrilla training camps and to establish a place for the headquarters of The Shield. Clendenning also donated money to brother militia elements in an attempt to unify the various patriotic groups. John Barrone began making plans to hit the Brink's main vault in San Francisco, an operation which would have netted the staggering sum of $50 million. Only a tip from a traitor, which alerted the FBI and made the heist impossible, prevented the robbery from taking place.

During the Brink's job, Clendenning dropped a pistol, which allowed the FBI to trace it to the mailbox of another Shield member. At the same time, Shield member Thomas Martin was arrested in St. Louis for passing counterfeit money. Martin betrayed his vows and his race, agreeing to become a government informant. He flew to Seattle, Washington, to meet with Clendenning and John Barrone.

Agents raided the hotel the next morning. Clendenning could have killed one of the officers, but he spared his life, only wounding him, before he himself was wounded. John Barrone, who had already made good his own escape, returned to rescue Clendenning.

Recognizing his mistake, Clendenning vowed to never be merciful again. The FBI traced Clendenning to Wheeler County in the Blue Mountains of Oregon, where brave members of The Shield fought a courageous battle against Federal agents, holding their own until the government firebombed the house. By then Emma Clenden-

*ning, the mother of all warriors for truth, had been
killed, and Luke Clendenning was grievously wounded.
Clendenning ordered John Barrone to make good his
escape. As Barrone was sneaking through the woods behind the house, he heard Clendenning keeping up a
steady fire against the federal agents, even as he was
being burned alive.*

*With that battle, The Shield ceased to exist as a viable
group. John Barrone, who with Luke Clendenning's
death would have become the head of The Shield, had
The Shield survived, remains at large.*

Felix Coker let out a low whistle.

"Jesus! We've got ourselves a real hero here," he
said under his breath.

There were several photos included with the text,
and Felix Coker printed out both the text and the
pictures.

Back at the Code Team Headquarters, Don Yee
chuckled. What Felix Coker did not know was that the
Website he had just viewed was nonexistent. It was actually no more than a very sophisticated e-mail that
gave the illusion of being a Website, but only to the
computer Felix Coker was using.

THIRTEEN

Heart of Dothan Motel, Dothan, Alabama

Chris Neighbors was sitting at the table near the windows. Bob Jeeter was propped up against the pillows on one of the two queen-sized beds in the room. At the moment, he was flipping through the TV channels.

Just outside their motel room some kids were playing in the swimming pool, and the happy scream of one of them penetrated through the low rumbling sound of the air-conditioner.

Chris reached into the sack on the table, took out a peanut, and popped it into his mouth, shell and all, just as Bob had told him to do. When he bit down on the peanut shell, he was surprised by the gush of salt water that spilled into his mouth. But that wasn't the only surprise. Instead of being hard and crispy as he'd expected, the peanut was soft and mushy.

"Damn!" Chris said, making a face and spitting out the peanut, shell and all. "What the hell did you say these things were?"

"Boiled peanuts," Bob Garrett answered. "Only around here, you have to call them 'balled' peanuts." Bob had his own sack, and he popped one of them into his mouth.

"What do you do with the shell?"

"You don't eat the shell," Bob explained. "You bite down on the shell, then pull the peanuts out with your tongue. Discard the shell." Demonstrating, Bob pulled the shell halves from his mouth and put them in an ashtray. "Then eat the peanuts." Bob smacked his lips appreciatively.

"God, how can you eat these slimy things?"

"It's like eating caviar," Bob said. "You have to acquire a taste."

"No, it's not, by God, like eating caviar," Chris said. "Which, by the way, I don't like either."

Bob laughed. "Well, then, it *is* like eating caviar, isn't it?"

"Yeah, I guess if you put it like that, it is."

"I'm telling you, Chris, if you're going to hang out with these boys, you're going to have to learn to eat boiled peanuts," Bob said, popping another one into his mouth.

"How much longer are we going to have to hang around with this bunch of rednecked bastards anyway?" Chris asked. Making a face, he put another boiled peanut in his mouth. Carefully removing the shell, he managed to eat the nuts. "I mean, what made Don choose this group as a potential for Coldfire? Hell, I doubt there's anyone in the whole bunch who can even spell the words nuclear device, let alone get their hands on one."

"Don's research showed quite a bit of cross correspondence between this particular chapter and Freedom Nation. And Freedom Nation has been corresponding with the Website that has the nuke for sale."

The meeting of the Wiregrass Chapter of the Alabama Knights of the White Orchid was held in the back room of Belcher's Store. The members began arriving just before seven o'clock, mostly in pickup trucks, nearly all of which sported a Confederate stars and bars, either as the front license plate, or as a flag fluttering from the antenna. Most had gun racks in the back window. Those who arrived were dressed in jeans, coveralls, or khaki pants, though many were wearing a white pullover shirt with a logo over their left breast pocket. The logo was a burning cross in a red ellipse, flanked by horses rampant, each horse carrying a hooded and robed rider. Printed around the logo were the words "Alabama Knights of the White Orchid."

The men, ranging in age from early twenties to mid-sixties, greeted each other as they got out of their vehicles. Most went straight to the drink box, where they pulled out a beer. A couple of them sat on the edge of the porch with their legs dangling over the edge. One of them pulled out a sack of boiled peanuts, and the two of them began eating them. Bob and Chris were sitting in Bob's pickup truck, and Bob chuckled.

"I told you so," he said, nodding toward the two who were eating peanuts.

Seeing Bob and Chris still in their truck, Arnie came over to greet them.

"You boys come on in," he invited. "We're about to get started here."

Bob and Chris got out of the truck and followed Frank through the staring eyes of the others to the back of the store. The room at the back of the store was set up for the meeting, complete with a very large logo painted on the wall. Oddly, as they passed through the store itself, they saw a young black woman and her child making a purchase. The storeowner took a bag of lemon drops from his stock and handed it to the little black boy.

"Here you go, LeRoy. Don't say I never give you nothin'."

"LeRoy, you tell the man thank you now," the boy's

mother said, looking nervously at all the white men who were just now trouping through the store.

"Thank you, Mr. Belcher," LeRoy said.

"I spec's you better hurry on now, Miss Ford," Belcher said. "We about to start our meetin' here and I'll be closin' down the store."

"Yes, sir," Miss Ford replied, pushing LeRoy along in front of her.

Belcher followed Miss Ford to the front door, then closed it behind her. Locking the door, he turned the sign around so that it read CLOSED to anyone else who might show up.

"Hey, Belcher, you getting any of that?" one of the young men called out, and everyone else laughed.

"Hell, you know he is," one of the others said. "Didn't you get a good look at LeRoy? Why, that boy's the spittin' image of Belcher."

Again everyone laughed.

"All right, you guys, knock it off," Belcher said. "Ain't nothin' in the bylaws says I can't be nice to nigras. Hell, they half my business."

"Belcher's right," Arnie said. "Leave 'im be. He lets us meet here for nothin', don't he?"

"We was just funnin', that's all."

Arnie walked up to the front of the room, where he very solemnly placed a Bible on the podium. Then, flanked by the battle flag of the Confederacy as well as the Alabama state flag, he turned to face the group.

"It's time to get the meetin' started. Brother Brubaker, would you lead us in prayer?"

The man called Brubaker gave the invocation, but it was unlike any invocation Bob or Chris had ever heard. The prayer was for the ultimate victory of the white race over the lower races.

After the prayer, Arnie began the meeting by stating the precepts of Alabama Knights of the White Orchid.

"As usual, I begin by saying that membership in the

Alabama Knights of the White Orchid is open only to white, Aryan, non-Jewish, Caucasian, Teutonic, European-descended peoples. The term white, or Aryan, includes all fair-skinned peoples of European descent; including Irish, English, Scottish, Dutch, German, Scandinavian, Italian, French, Austrian, Polish, Slavic, Russian, etc. The terms white or Aryan do not refer to Asian, African, Jewish, Middle Eastern, Caribbean, South American, Latino, Hispanic, Mexican, or Pacific Islander, or any mixture between white and thereof. Australian or South African heritage is acceptable as these are descended from white European nations.

"Indians, and notice that I call them Indians and not Native Americans, are of Mongolian Asian stock and are not considered white. However, we will not be bogged down in arguments over who is part Indian and who is not. The bottom line is this. If you look white, act white, think white, and willing to fight for white rights, you are white."

"Damn right," Frank said from the audience, and several others mumbled their agreement.

"We do not accept nor will we tolerate habitual drunks, illegal drug use, homosexuals, child molesters, those previously convicted of sexual misconduct, or those in a previous or current interracial affair."

"Whoa, Belcher, there goes your chances with that good-lookin' nigra just left here," someone said, and while Belcher glared, a few laughed nervously.

Arnie stared with disapproval at the would-be jokester, as if addressing the final comment to him.

"No white trash will be tolerated. The original movement, led by General Nathan Bedford Forrest, was made up of dignified Southern gentlemen. All members should seek to emulate Brother Forrest and the dignity that he became famous for. The Alabama Knights of the White Orchid will strive to maintain this order. White decency will prevail."

"Hear, hear," the would-be jokester said, clapping his hands, then looking around at the others, urging their applause as well.

"Now, let us say together the Fourteen Words," Arnie said.

Standing and placing their hands over their hearts and facing the Confederate flag, the men recited in unison the mantra they called the Fourteen Words.

"We must secure the existence of our people, and a future for white children."

After that, the meeting quickly became as mundane as a meeting of a local library board. They discussed such things as a scheduled picnic, upcoming rallies by other White Orchid groups, and how much money they had in their treasury. According to the treasurer's report, they had $1,644.

Just as the meeting was about to be adjourned, Arnie said something that caused Bob and Chris to look at each other in interest.

"Hang on, my friends, hang on," Arnie said. "I can tell you now that a most powerful weapon will soon be in our hands, and when that day arrives, the mongrels of this nation will tremble before our wrath."

Fort Freedom, Missouri

That evening, showered and in clean uniforms, John and Jenny sat in a building known as Liberty Hall, along with over two hundred other uniformed men and women. They were gathered to hear their commander, General Lee Grant, speak.

"Have you ever heard General Grant speak?" a young woman sitting beside Jenny asked.

"Only on television," Jenny replied.

"Oh, you can't count that. Most of the time they

only take what they call a 'sound bite.' Wait until you really hear him. He is wonderful!"

The woman shook a little as she said the words, reminding Jenny of a much younger woman's girlish infatuation with a rock star.

"Have you been a member for a long time?" Jenny asked.

"I joined six months ago," the woman replied. "Since then I've been to two enbattlements."

"Enbattlements?"

"Training exercises for the civil war that is to come," the woman said. "You know, like today, when we crawled under live machine-gun fire on the infiltration course. I've learned to shoot guns, survive in the woods on snake and bugs, all sorts of things. It's much more exciting than the PTA," she said with a giggle.

"I'm sure it is," Jenny said.

Jenny turned her attention back toward the front of the room. The stage from which General Grant would speak was flanked with two flags, the Freedom Nation flag on one side, and on the other, another flag bearing two stars, which was the personal standard of General Grant.

Freedom Nation's flag was a bastardization of the original flag of the U.S. The blue field had a circle of thirteen white stars, just as the original U.S. flag did, but in the center of the thirteen stars was a white swastika. Superimposed over the red and white stripes was an arm, holding a blood-dripping sword.

Behind the stage there was a larger-than-life poster of a man and woman in the uniform known as battle-dress utilities, complete with helmet. The new helmets looked, Jenny thought, startlingly like the drop-sided German helmets of World War II. The poster figures were each clutching an M-16 rifle, and the message on the poster read: THE PRICE OF FREEDOM IS ETERNAL VIGILANCE!

After studying all the trappings of the room for a while, Jenny looked around at the others who had filed in to listen to Grant speak. She and John had been at the Fort Freedom militia camp for a couple of days now, and had met many, if not most, of the militiamen. The number of former military men who belonged to the militia didn't surprise her, but she was surprised by the others: the shopkeepers and accountants, the farmers and mechanics, the students and the housewives, the old and the young.

"Attenhut!" someone shouted from the back of the room.

There was a scrape of chairs as everyone responded to the shouted order. General Grant entered the room from the rear, then hurried quickly up the aisle toward the front. He hopped energetically onto the stage, then strolled over toward the podium.

"Thank you, as you were," he said.

There was another scrape of chairs as everyone in the room retook their seats.

Someone coughed.

An air conditioner kicked on.

Grant stepped out from behind the podium and moved down to the front of the platform. He stood there for a long moment, letting his arms hang down, holding his hands together in front of him. He made an impressive picture, Jenny thought, with his tall, militarily erect body, silver hair, and bronzed skin. He didn't ask for quiet, nor did he raise his hands in signal. Nevertheless, the scores of conversations stilled and the room grew quiet, save for the occasional clearing of a throat, scrape of a chair, or the soft hum of the air conditioner.

Grant had been looking down at the floor all this time, as if in prayer. He kept the people waiting, even beyond the point at which they had grown silent, effectively building the tension. Finally, he looked up and let his ice-blue eyes rake across everyone present, making eye contact with most of them.

Like the others in the assembly hall, Grant was in uniform, though his uniform differed in that he was wearing general's stars on the collar and ribbons above the left breast pocket. Technically, the rank was now bogus, for Grant had been reduced to colonel when he was forced into retirement. But the ribbons, Jenny knew, were real, for Arlington Lee Grant was a highly decorated veteran of both the war in Vietnam and the Gulf War.

"My fellow warriors for freedom," General Grant began. He spoke very quietly, his words barely more than a mumble, and even from the front row, Jenny had to strain to hear him.

There were a few more scraping sounds as chairs were repositioned, a cough, and some nervous shushing.

"It is now a dark and dismal time in the history of our race. All about us lie the green graves of our sires, yet in a land once ours, we have become a people dispossessed.

"Look around you, and what do you see? You see an America filled with hatred and contempt and fear and loathing and rage . . . and depravity, piled upon depravity."

So far Grant's voice had been soft, caressing . . . almost sensual, and the words "depravity, piled upon depravity" were little more than a sibilant whisper.

General Grant stood silently for a long moment. His eyes closed, as if he were summoning inspiration from deep within. Then he continued, only a little louder than before.

"By the millions, those not of our blood violate our borders and mock our claim to sovereignty. Mexicans by the legion invade our soil while we murder our babies in equal numbers. Our heroes and our culture have been insulted and degraded.

"Throughout this land our children are being coerced into accepting nonwhites for their idols, their companions, and worst of all their mates. This is a course which is taking us straight to oblivion.

"Evidence abounds that a certain vile, alien people have taken control of our country. All about us the land is dying. Our cities swarm with dusky hordes. The water is rancid and the air is rank. The coloreds of this world pick gleefully at our bones while the Jews, those vile hook-nosed masters of usury, orchestrate our destruction.

"Evil is upon us!" he suddenly shouted, his voice cracking over the head of his audience like a peal of thunder.

"And I say this to the liberal sycophants . . . the brown-nosing toadies of ZOG . . . the Zionist Occupied Government. Listen to me!"

Now he was at the peak of his form, booming the challenge loudly, his words echoing back from the four corners of the assembly hall.

"We will make your so-called New World Order pay for every family you invade, we will make you pay for every farm you steal, and we will make you pay for every life you ruin! You will pay in violence and pain and anguish until the ground is red with blood and soaked in the tears of our beleaguered race. We, the Euro-Christians who are the *true* custodians of this nation, will not go quietly into the night! We will make war in whatever way it takes to preserve the liberties our forefathers won for us. We will choke you and your kind until you cannot breathe! And we . . . will . . . win!"

"We will . . ." someone shouted.

"WIN!" the group responded.

"We will . . ."

"WIN!"

"We will . . ."

"WIN!"

The decibel level increased with each full-throated response until it was as if the very windows would shatter from the noise. Grant nodded approvingly, then held up his hand, and the room grew instantly quiet. He continued his speech.

"To all Euro-Christian men, women, and children of America, in the name of the Christian Yahweh, I ask you to examine that secret part of your heart wherein is born all that is good, and noble, and true, and ask yourself if you can respond as did Patrick Henry so long ago! If you can, then say those words with me now. But don't say them unless you can speak with a clear conscience and resolute spirit. 'Give me liberty, or give me death!' "

"Liberty or death! Liberty or death! Liberty or death!" the audience replied, shouting at the top of their voices and leaping to their feet in unbridled enthusiasm.

The general left the stage then, moving quickly down the center aisle toward the door. From both sides of the aisle people pushed toward him to reach out and shake his hand or, barring that, to at least touch him. Not until he was gone did the hubbub subside.

"Ladies and gentlemen, Elvis has left the building," John said quietly.

Jenny laughed.

FOURTEEN

Detroit

The building had once been a store, and the walls were still lined with display shelves, racks, and cabinets. A few faded posters advertised goods long absent from the premises, such as R.C. Cola and Ipana Toothpaste. Despite these outdated trappings of mercantilism, Paul knew he was in the right place because a sign in front of the building made the grandiose pronouncement that this was the NATIONAL HEADQUARTERS OF THE OPPRESSED BROTHERHOOD.

Paul held the door open for Linda, then stepped in behind her. They were met by two large men, one of whom had adopted the style of hair and dress of the Hollywood actor Mr. T. The other man had a flattened nose, scar tissue over both his eyes, and a permanent scowl. He looked like half the defensive linemen Paul had ever played against.

"You packin'?" Mr. T asked.

"Hell, yes, I'm packin'," Paul said.

Mr. T held out his hand. "Give it to me."

"Fuck you, I'm not givin' up my piece."

"You want to talk to the Man, you got to give up your gun. You don't want to do that, then get the fuck out of here."

"Give 'im your gun, baby," Linda said. "We don't want no trouble."

"Better listen to your pussy, man," Mr. T said. "I ain't somebody you want to mess with."

Paul stared at the two big men for a moment, then with a shrug, pulled his pistol from his inside jacket pocket. He handed it over to Mr. T.

Mr. T smiled, then turned the gun around and pointed it back at Paul's forehead.

"Lesson number one," Mr. T said. "Never give up your piece. What if I was some honky-assed cop? I could shoot you now."

"Lesson number two," Paul replied. "Never point a gun at someone unless you are actually willing to pull the trigger."

"You think I'm not willing to pull the trigger?" Mr. T asked.

"Pull it."

"Say what?"

"Pull the trigger, you fat pig, or I'm going to take that gun away from you and shove it up your ass."

Mr. T looked shocked. "You a crazy motherfucker, you know that?"

"Pull the trigger!" Paul demanded.

With a ferocious shout, Mr. T pulled the trigger. It made a clicking sound.

"What?" Mr. T asked, looking at the pistol.

Paul grinned broadly. "Lesson number three. If you're going to pull the trigger, make sure it's loaded." Holding up his hand, Paul opened his palm to show the magazine he had slipped from the pistol before handing it over to Mr. T.

"I don't need no gun to take care of your ass," Mr. T shouted. He lunged toward Paul. Adroitly, Paul stepped aside, then brought the knife-edge of his hand down in a karate chop to the back of Mr. T's neck. Mr. T went down.

The lineman started after Paul then, but he took only one step before Linda whirled around, sending her foot whistling out in a smashing blow to the lineman's leg. Holding his knee and howling in pain, the lineman went down as well.

"Holy shit," a voice said.

Looking toward a door that led into a back room, Paul and Linda saw Ibo Mogombi. "How'd you do that?"

"Wasn't all that hard," Paul said. He pointed to the two men, who were just now beginning to get up. "If that's the best you've got, you ain't got much."

"You caught me by surprise," Mr. T said, rubbing the back of his neck. "Now let's see what you've really got."

"Linda, would you handle it?" Paul asked, speaking as calmly as if asking her to hand him a cup of coffee.

"Sure thing, baby," Linda replied just as calmly. Doing a quick pirouette, she kicked Mr. T in the chin. He went down again.

Ibo Mogombi laughed, and clapped his hands slowly. "That's pretty damn good," he said. "Come on back here, I'll introduce you to the Man."

Paul and Linda followed Ibo through the door. This smaller chamber, perhaps once a storeroom, was now a showplace of tapestries, animal skins, and African art: from masks to stylized ebony figurines in various poses.

A huge man sat behind a table in the middle of the room. He wasn't big the way Mr. T and the lineman were big. They were muscular. This man was fat, with huge, fleshy jowls, an oversized neck, and enormous girth. He had two plates in front of him. One plate was filled with barbecued spare ribs; the other was piled over with cleaned bones. He was working on a rib as Ibo brought Paul and Linda in to meet him, and pieces of greasy meat hung from his lips and several rows of chins. Two young, svelte, and very pretty women were with him, one on each side. Solicitously, one of the women cleaned his chin with a wet cloth, while the other dabbed a towel against it.

"This is Kwazi Bin Falazi," Ibo said, holding his hand out toward the big man.

"I'm sorry about interrupting your dinner," Paul said.

"Ain't my dinner," Kwazi replied. "It's just a snack." Kwazi looked at Linda, then back at Paul. "What's the matter? You couldn't find yourself a woman with a little more of the brush? That one's so damn yella she probably glows in the dark."

The two women with Kwazi, both of whom were the color of lightly creamed coffee, laughed, then leaned possessively against the big man.

"She's all right," Paul said. "I don't hold who her mama slept with against her."

"Your daddy a white man?" Kwazi asked Linda.

"So my mama says."

"You know who he is?"

"Dan Quayle," Linda said.

Kwazi looked at her for a moment as if shocked by her answer, then laughed out loud. "Dan Quayle," he said. "Like the man said, you all right." He tore off a piece of meat and held it toward her. "Want some rib?"

"No, thanks," Linda said. "I'm trying to keep my girlish figure."

"Yeah, you do that." Kwazi stuck the meat in his own mouth. "So, you're interested in joining the Oppressed Brotherhood, are you?" he asked, turning his attention back toward Paul.

"No, not especially. Who told you that?"

Kwazi looked at Ibo in surprise. "What kind of shit you pullin' on me, man?" he asked. "I thought you tole me he wanted to join."

"I said he would be a good man," Ibo replied quickly. "And once he figures out who we are and what we are about, why, he'll want to join up for sure."

"What makes you think he would be a good man?"

"He and Fine Shine here took down Dooley and Pig Meat," Ibo said.

"What do you mean, took 'em down?"

Ibo pointed over his shoulder. "They back in there right now nursin' their wounds," he said. "Clark took Dooley down, his woman took down Pig Meat."

"The woman took down Pig Meat?"

"Yes. And Dooley, when Dooley tried to get back up."

"Ain't that the shits, now?" Kwazi asked, laughing. He looked at Paul. "Look here, bro, we could use people like you and sister here. So tell me, why don't you want to join the Oppressed Brotherhood?"

"I don't know anything about you but the name of your group," Paul said. "And I have to tell you, that doesn't do anything for me."

"What you mean?"

"You call yourselves the Oppressed Brotherhood? To have a name like that is the same then as saying"—Paul affected a Stepin Fetchit accent before continuing—*"Yassuh, Mista White Folk. Ya'll come on and does anything you wants to me now. I jus' be a po' downtrodden oppressed colored man, so they ain't nothin' I can do about it, 'ceptin' maybe kiss yo' ass iffen you wants me to."*

Kwazi chuckled. "So, you think we're just goin' to roll over for Whitey? Is that it?"

"That's what your name says," Paul said.

"Ibo, step out and let me have a few words with these people. Take my ladies with you."

"You be all right if I leave you alone with 'em?" Ibo asked, looking at Paul and Linda.

"You mean, are they goin' come down on my black ass?" Kwazi asked.

"Well, yeah, somethin' like that," Ibo agreed.

"Well, now, tell me, my man, if they want to do that while you in here, you goin' stop 'em? I mean, if they be as bad as you say?"

"No, I guess not," Ibo admitted.

Kwazi motioned for Ibo to leave. When the women didn't go with Ibo, Kwazi looked up at them. "You, too," he said.

"Baby, what we got to go for?"

" 'Cause I say," Kwazi replied.

Pouting, the women left with Ibo. Kwazi waited until they were gone and the door shut before he spoke again.

"You two interest me," he said. "I think you would be a real asset to our organization, yet you say you don't want to join because you disapprove of our name. Tell me, young man. Just what would you have us call ourselves?"

Paul noticed a striking change in the syntax of Kwazi's language, both in pattern and vocabulary. He sounded considerably less like a street tough, and more like James Earl Jones.

"I don't know. Something that isn't quite so submissive."

"Something like the Black Panthers perhaps? Or maybe the New African Liberation Front? How about the Symbionese Liberation Army?" Kwazi asked.

"At least those names show strength."

Kwazi held up his finger. "Oh, I am willing to concede that the names do suggest a certain degree of strength. But consider the organizations to which those names are attached. They are either gone, or are powerless. The Black Panthers? Nostalgia. Oh, I admit, there's a group trying to call themselves that now, but they are impostors. None of the present pretenders were even born when Bobby Seale, Huey Newton, Eldridge Cleaver, and Julius Markham were

manning the barricades in the turbulent sixties. And
the Symbionese Liberation Army? Well, we all know
what happened to Cinque and his little group of misguided heroes, don't we? We watched them perish in
a fire, long before the Branch Davidians entered into
their own martyrdom. What about the New African
Liberation Front? Who are they? Are they marching
in the streets? Are they being pursued by police dogs,
getting their heads broken by nightsticks, being jailed
for their beliefs? No, their battleground is the sterile
atmosphere of the Internet. The New African Liberation Front is nothing more than a Website that bleeds
our brothers by continually asking for donations. Hell,
I wouldn't be surprised if the site was run by a couple
of teenaged white computer geeks, using the money
they raise to buy more computer equipment.

"Now, let us consider the Oppressed Brotherhood.
We, my friend, are a viable organization."

"You call yourselves a viable organization, yet you
meet in a storefront," Paul said.

"We are an urban guerrilla army, so we find an urban hideout. Castro met in caves before he took over
Cuba."

"You think you can take over America?" Paul asked.

"We don't need to take over the entire country. We
need only to carve out a bit for ourselves."

"Even that is ambitious."

"Nothing worthwhile is ever done without ambition."

"Ambition, without the wherewithal to bring it off,
is a waste of effort," Paul said.

"We have the wherewithal," Kwazi said. "Or at least,
we soon will have."

"Yes, I met some of your wherewithal," Paul said,
nodding toward the front of the store.

"Obviously, you know that I don't mean them,

though I think we should talk about them again in a few moments."

"Mr. Falazi, I can't help but notice that there has been a marked change in your speech pattern," Paul said.

Kwazi laughed. "Have you, now?"

"You want to explain that to me?"

"I am a chameleon, Mr. Clark. I adapt to my surroundings. If a certain ghetto patois serves my needs better than boardroom English, then I will use ghetto patois. You seem to be an educated man. Are you a college graduate?"

"Yes."

"As am I," Kwazi said. "In fact, Mr. Clark, at one time I was a political science professor at Stanford University."

"You taught political science? Wait a minute. One of the early Black Panthers was a poly-sci professor from Stanford, wasn't he?"

"You know your history."

"You? You are Julius Markham?"

"In the flesh," Kwazi said. He laughed at himself. "And as you can see, there is quite a bit of my flesh now. I don't blame you for not recognizing me. I bear absolutely no resemblance to that fiery, young, slender man who was so often seen on television."

"I've often wondered what happened to you. I knew you didn't go to prison, nor leave the country."

"In my case, neither option was necessary. Other than a few disturbing-the-peace and parading-without-a-permit violations, the police never had cause to prosecute. On the other hand, I had, quite effectively, managed to cut my own throat. My activities were so controversial that Stanford was able to overcome my tenure and terminate my services."

"I've read about you," Paul said. "As I recall, you

had been chosen as one of the nation's top ten college professors."

"Yes, our country does like top-ten lists, doesn't it?"

"My point is, you were so smart and so well regarded that when you left Stanford you could have gone anywhere you liked, couldn't you?"

"I'm afraid not. Within the academic circles, I became persona non grata."

"And now you have become, what? Head of a gang of militant brothers?"

"One does what one must do," Kwazi said. "But don't let my cynicism mislead you. I do believe in the cause. I always have, and I always will."

"And you really think this little group of people can have some impact on the way things are?" Paul asked.

"I do indeed. Mr. Clark, a short while ago you asked about our wherewithal. You are an educated man. Do you know the significance of the formula E equals MC squared?"

"Sure, it's Einstein's theory dealing with the amount of energy contained in an atom. It was the basis for . . . holy shit! Are you telling me that you have . . ."

Kwazi held up his hand, cutting Paul off in midsentence.

"I'm not saying that we do," Kwazi said. "But neither am I closing the door to that possibility."

"How the hell are you going to get your hands on a nuke? I mean, that is what you are talking about, isn't it? Getting a nuclear weapon of some sort?"

"I seem to have piqued your interest," Kwazi said.

"Hell, yes, I'm interested."

"Interested enough to join?"

"We'll both join right now, if you want us."

"Ah, good, the ball is in my court again," Kwazi said. "You are asking to join, and only I have the power to grant you membership. But first, I need to satisfy my curiosity about something."

"Sure. Ask anything you want."

"Why ask, when I can have an empirical demonstration," Kwazi replied. "Ibo! Dooley! Pig Meat! Get in here!" he bellowed.

Ibo and the two big men came rushing in as if they were responding to a call for help. When they saw Kwazi sitting calmly behind his table, they stopped short. The two women came in as well, and they stopped just inside the door, looking on anxiously.

"Everything all right, Mr. Falazi?" Ibo asked.

"Maybe I should ask those two if everything is all right," Kwazi replied, waving his hand toward the two big men.

Pig Meat was still showing a slight limp, and Dooley, the one Paul had nicknamed Mr. T, now had a Band-Aid on his chin.

"Do Ibo be tellin' me the truth? You let these two take you down?" Kwazi's speech pattern had returned to what he had referred to as ghetto patois.

"They caught us by surprise, Mr. Falazi," Dooley explained. "I mean, one minute we was getting ready to bring 'em in to see you, and the next minute, out of the blue, they started pulling some of that karate shit on us."

Kwazi banged his hand down on the table so hard that the plate full of bones fell to the floor. "You two supposed to be my bodyguards, motherfuckers! You ain't supposed to be surprised by nobody!"

"We wasn't expectin' nothin'," Dooley said. "It won't happen again."

"Oh, you mighty right 'bout it ain't goin' to happen again," Kwazi said. " 'Cause I just got myself a couple new bodyguards." He looked at Paul and Linda. "You want to be my bodyguards?"

"Sure, why not?" Paul replied. "I wouldn't want to

join the group, then have something happen to you right after I joined."

"Come on, Mr. Falazi, you shittin' us? You can't mean you want a woman be your bodyguard? I mean, what the fuck can she do to protect you?"

"Let's find out," Kwazi said. "You two come after me. Girl, you protect me. Not you," he added to Paul. He looked back at Linda. "Just you."

"What do you mean, come after you?" Dooley asked.

"What you think I mean, fool? I said come after me. Try 'n hit me over the head, cut my throat, shoot me. Try anything you want. I want to see can this girl stop you."

Dooley held his hands, palm-out, toward Kwazi. "No, now, you don't want that, Mr. Falazi. I mean, you know she can't do nothin' to protect you, and I don't want to hurt you."

"Attack me," Kwazi said. "Both of you. Come get me."

"No, I can't . . . we can't," Dooley demurred.

"Ibo, pull your gun," Kwazi ordered coldly. "If these two don't try and attack me, I mean *really* try and attack me, shoot them."

Ibo pulled his pistol and pointed it at Dooley and Pig Meat. "You heard what the man say," he said. "You better take him down." Making little motioning movements with his pistol, he indicated that they should attack.

Pig Meat and Dooley looked at each other for no more than half a second. Then Dooley leaned over and whispered something to Pig Meat. Pig Meat smiled, and with a roar of defiance, Pig Meat started toward Linda, while Dooley started toward Kwazi.

Ducking to one side, Linda sent her foot into the side of Pig Meat's other knee, kicking this knee even harder than she had the other one. With a roar of pain, Pig Meat went down.

Even as Linda was jamming her foot into the side of Pig Meat's knee, she was shooting her hand forward, fist doubled, toward Dooley. She could break cinder blocks with this same blow—and often did. But this time her target wasn't cinder blocks. This time her target was Dooley's balls.

Dooley's yell of pain filled the room.

Linda moved quickly to put herself between Kwazi and his two would-be attackers. She assumed a karate position, waiting for Dooley and Pig Meat's next move.

Slowly, the two straightened up. Neither was seriously hurt, but the expressions on their faces were contorted with pain. For a moment they looked as if they might try to continue the attack, but by now, Linda was clearly in the on-guard position.

"Ahh, fuck you, bitch," Dooley finally said, using his hand to wave off any additional attacks. "You win. I ain't goin' try no more."

Nursing their wounds and shaking their heads, Dooley and Pig Meat turned and walked away.

"Damn," Kwazi said. "I ain't never seen nothin' like that 'cept in the movies." He looked at Paul. "You as good as she is?"

"I'm better."

"Might be fun to see you prove it," Kwazi said.

Paul smiled drolly, then shook his head. "You don't want to see that," he said.

"Why not?"

"She's too good for me to beat."

"What you mean, she's too good for you beat? I thought you just said you was better."

"I am better," Paul said. "But she's so good that the only way I could beat her is kill her. And I'm not going to kill my woman just to please you, bodyguard job or not."

"On the other hand, I might kill *you*," Linda said.

"True," Paul agreed.

"Damn! Ain't you two somethin' now?" Kwazi asked. "Don't worry, don't worry, ain't goin' to have you kill one another. I just want you to be my bodyguards, that's all."

"That we can do," Paul said.

FIFTEEN

Fort Freedom, Missouri

"I was just a captain then," General Grant was saying. He was hosting a meal in his command quarters, and the table was spread with a white linen cloth and set with fine china on gold chargers flanked by exquisite crystal and ornate silverware. "But I understood the concept of total war better than any of my commanders, all the way up to and including my then-commander in chief."

General Grant, who was wearing a white dress-mess uniform complete with miniature medals, got up from the table and walked over to the buffet. He pulled a bottle of wine from a silver ice bucket, then looked over at Jenny.

"More brandy, my dear?" he asked.

"Yes, thank you. It is excellent, by the way."

Grant cradled the bottle in his hand as he examined the label. "It should be. This was bottled especially for Napoleon. I came by it when I was club officer for the NATO Officers' Club in Brussels." He brought the bottle over to the table and poured more wine for both Jenny and John. He didn't offer any to any of the others who were sharing the table with them. They too were in uniform, but like John and Jenny, they were wearing the ubiquitous camouflaged battle-dress utilities. Only Arlington Lee Grant was dressed in splendor.

"You were telling us how you interrogated prisoners in Vietnam, General," John said.

"Ah, yes," Grant said, resuming his place at the head of the table. "We had taken three prisoners, and it was vital that we get some information from them. I was company executive officer of the 86th Helicopter Attack Company. We were on the verge of launching a major operation and we needed to know the location of the VC brigade. Otherwise, we could have flown right into an ambush. Helicopter insertions look good when you see them on TV on the History Channel, but let me tell you from having made more than my share of them, they were hairy operations. You never knew if you were just going to set down and let your troops off, or fly into such a heavy concentration of fire that you would be knocked down like flies. My commander wanted to know the location of the VC brigade. I felt like I *must* know the location. So I was determined to get the information by whatever means it took. And if it meant being . . . forceful . . . in the prisoner interrogation, than that is exactly what I intended to do."

Grant paused in his discourse long enough to take a drink of the brandy. He smacked his lips in appreciation, then continued his story.

"The ranking VC prisoner was a lieutenant who had great command presence. He wouldn't break, and he held the others to the same standard. Our battalion S-2 had been unable to get anything from them, so I was ordered to take them up to Division for further interrogation. But as I said, my personal need to know was great enough that I didn't want to leave it up to those incompetents at Division. So I took charge of the prisoners at 0900 hours, and by 0930 I was back in the colonel's CP with all the information he needed."

"You were able to make them talk when the others couldn't? How?" Jenny asked.

Grant set his brandy snifter down in front of him, put his elbows on the table, and clasped his hands just under his chin. He looked directly at Jenny as he answered her question.

"I put all three of them in the back of a three-quarter-ton truck. As soon as we were out of sight of the battalion base camp, I stopped the truck, then ordered the three prisoners to disembark. Once they were all out of the truck, I pulled my pistol and aimed it at their leader. Through my interpreter, I asked him to tell me where the VC were."

"And he told you?"

Grant shook his head no. "No. As I said, he was an excellent soldier and a fine officer. He was a worthy opponent, and I had a lot of admiration and respect for him. He had seen it all before, of course, the empty threats we often made trying to force them to talk. He was so positive that this was also an empty threat that he stared down the barrel of the pistol and laughed."

"So, what did you do?"

"Oh, I pulled the trigger, my dear," Grant said easily. "Sergeant Major Clay, would you pass the butter, please?"

Clay passed the butter to Grant, who proceeded to spread it on his roll.

"You pulled the trigger?" Jenny asked.

"I did indeed. I shot him right between the eyes."

"What did the others do?" one of the men at the table asked.

Grant laughed. "Now, that was the beautiful thing," he said. "Almost before their lieutenant's body hit the

180   *William W. Johnstone*

ground, they were yelling out the information I needed."

"So, what did you do with them?" John asked.

"Why, I didn't do anything with them. I let them go."

"You let them go? On your own initiative?" John asked.

"Yes, on my own initiative. By doing that, I was able to use them to serve a greater purpose. You see, they had just seen a vivid demonstration of the art of the carrot and stick. I killed one prisoner because he wouldn't cooperate with me—that was the stick—and I freed those who did cooperate with me. That was the carrot. Can you imagine what sort of message that sent? I wanted these two to be able to spread the word so that if I encountered the situation again, it would be easier to extract information. And in fact that is just what happened. For the next several weeks, everyone we captured could hardly wait to spill their guts."

"And, of course, you derived an added bonus from letting them go," John suggested.

"An added bonus? I don't understand," Grant replied. "What sort of added bonus?"

"By setting them free, there would be little danger of them turning you in for murdering a prisoner, would there?"

"Murdering a prisoner?" one of the others at the table asked, his voice raised in protest. "What do you mean, murdering?" This was Elliot Keefer, Grant's second in command. So far as John could determine, though, the position of second in command was little more than a title. All power rested in the hands of General Arlington Lee Grant.

"You don't think it is considered murder to kill a prisoner who is in your charge?" John asked.

"I don't think it should be classified as murder unless you kill a human being," Keefer said. "And as far as I'm concerned, no slant-eyed yellow monkey is a human, whether he be Vietnamese, Chinese, or Jap."

"Yeah," one of the others said. "They're no better than a nigger."

"Don't forget the hook-nosed Jews," another said.

"And the wetbacks. All those Mexican bastards coming across the Rio Grande to take good American jobs."

"You mean like plucking chickens and picking fruit?" Jennifer asked.

Grant shot a glance of disapproval toward Jenny, and John kicked her under the table.

"What about the Iraqis and Iranians?" one of the others said.

"You can ask Mr. Barrone about that," General Grant said, smiling at John. "He, Sergeant Major Clay, and I were, in fact, the first Americans to invade Iraq." Grant then went on to tell the story of their night incursion to take out General Sin-Sargon.

"Yeah, well, it's too bad we just killed Iraqis during that war," Keefer said. "Far as I'm concerned they're all alike. All the towel-heads. I'd just as soon see them all dead."

"And the Indians," another put in.

"Yeah, both kinds of Indians, the ones from India and our own homegrown variety."

"Don't forget the statue-praying, Pope-led, Mary-worshiping Catholics."

"Yeah, and the Canadians," John added.

"Canadians?" Keefer asked, surprised by John's comment.

"Hell, yes, the Canadians," John replied. "They've stolen two of our baseball teams, they've screwed up the rules for football, they dominate our hockey teams, and half of them are damn frogs anyway."

"Are we against the Canadians?" Keefer asked in confusion.

General Grant smiled. "I think our friend John is having a little fun at your expense. Am I right, Mr. Barrone?"

"I'm sorry. I thought everyone would know I was teasing," John said. He held up his glass. "To freedom."

"To freedom!" the others repeated. All drank the toast, but Jenny saw Elliot Keefer and one of the others exchange glances, then glare at John over the rims of their glasses. It was obvious that they were jealous of John's previous association with Grant and feared for their own positions in the group.

After dinner the guests adjourned to the den, where General Grant showed a video.

"I just got this back from a professional filmmaker," Grant explained as he picked up the remote and clicked on the giant-screen TV. "I saw it when they were putting it together, of course, but I haven't seen it in its final form. I'd like to know what you think about it. I plan to use it as a recruitment tool."

The opening scene was of Vietnam. There were pictures of infantrymen engaged in battle and of wounded soldiers being evacuated. A silken-voiced announcer provided the voice-over.

"During the war in Vietnam, white Americans shed red blood in the green jungle of a country best left to the yellow peoples who lived there. It was the wrong war at the wrong time and in the wrong place, yet many brave young Americans fought and died there.

"And what was happening on the streets of the very country for which these men were fighting and dying?"

Now the screen showed American cities in turmoil; the Watts riot, angry people spitting on soldiers in uniform and throwing rocks and bricks at military buses that were clearly marked with a red cross. Although there were whites in the crowd, the majority of protesters on screen were black.

"Urged on by the very dregs of our country, the Zionist Occupied Government caved in. They refused to support our brave fighting men while, at the same time, defending the rights of Americans to commit treason."

The screen showed Jane Fonda looking through the sights of a North Vietnamese antiaircraft gun.

"The ideals and freedoms espoused by the Founding Fathers have been discarded. There is now a new order of political correctness with a Zionist-inspired agenda to confiscate land from the hardworking farmers, levy unfair taxes on the workers, and redistribute money to the lower classes in exchange for their votes."

The pictures on screen portrayed farm auctions and closed businesses interspersed with smiling politicians moving through crowds of blacks.

"Those men and women who now hold high political office have lost sight of the one fundamental element of survival of any nation. And that is that the organic founding law of a nation must state with unmistakable and irrevocable specificity the identity of the homogeneous racial and cultural group for whose welfare it was formed. The continued existence of the nation is, singularly and for all time, for the welfare of that specific group only."

Now the picture on screen was filled with smiling faces of white men and women gathered in organizations and rallies under banners and posters proclaiming the Freedom Nation.

"Out of the ashes of this failed American experiment has risen Freedom Nation. Dedicated to the God-given right of the Aryan Christian Protestant to 'secure the existence of our people, and a future for white children,' Freedom Nation stands as a beacon to the world. And to command that battle, to assume the mantle of leadership of Freedom Nation, we have chosen a man who is a hero in every sense of the word."

Now the screen filled with the heroic image of Arlington Lee Grant. Behind him the flag of the United States morphed into the stars and stripes, swastika, and fist-gripped sword of Freedom Nation. The presentation closed by holding a full-screen view of that flag, then going to black.

To the applause and cheers of those who had gathered to watch the tape, Grant punched off the TV.

"What do you think?" he asked.

"It's wonderful, General!" Keefer said.

"Magnificent!" another insisted.

"Great!" others added.

Grant looked directly at John and Jenny. "Your enthusiasm seems strangely subdued."

John didn't realize that his disgust with the tape had been so evident. He had to think quickly.

"Oh, I thought the tape was great," he said. "I was just thinking of Lucas Clendenning. As I'm sure you are aware, General, Luke was one of the early patriots, someone who I am sure will be regarded as a founding father when our new order is established."

"Yes," Grant said. "Yes, of course. Well, it's too late to include a tribute to him in this tape. Copies have already been sent to television stations all over the country. But I'm sure this will generate a groundswell of support for our cause, and when it does, there will be opportunities to make new tapes and we will pay homage then."

"I'm sure he would be pleased," John said. "He was a strong believer in using propaganda to persuade the will of the people."

"Yes, well, there is a time for propaganda and a

time for action," Grant replied. "And the time for action is upon us."

"Oh?" John replied. "What makes you say that? Do you have something planned?"

"Yes. A little trip to St. Louis."

"What's so significant about St. Louis?"

"Nothing that I can talk about at this time," Grant said. "But when it happens, the message will be loud and clear."

Much later that night John and Jenny took a walk through the compound. John had already found two hidden mikes in his room, one in the telephone and another behind the ceiling light fixture. Jenny had turned up a couple of her own, and both were sure that there were probably several others around, not only in their rooms but in other gathering places. As a result, the only place they felt safe to talk was out in the open.

"I can't believe you ever actually admired this man," Jenny said.

"He was a good soldier," John replied.

"There's more to life than being a good soldier," Jenny insisted.

"Do you think the trip to St. Louis has anything to do with Coldfire?" she asked.

"I don't know, but I think we should assume that it does. I'm afraid if I push for an answer, though, he'll get suspicious."

"Halt!" The sudden shout, so close as it was, startled them. John and Jenny stopped in their tracks. A moment later a guard, his face smeared with camouflage paint, stepped out of the darkness. He was holding an M-16 rifle at the ready. "Who goes there?" the guard asked.

"I'm John Barrone. This is Jenny. We're new."

"You got a pass?" the guard asked.

"A pass?"

"You ain't supposed to be out on the grounds at night without a pass."

John and Jenny looked at each other, then back at the guard.

"Nobody said anything to us about a pass."

"Stay right there until I check on you."

The guard made a call on his radio. A moment later word came back that John and Jenny were all right, but they were advised to return to their quarters.

Putting away his radio, he looked up. "He said you . . ."

"Are supposed to return to our quarters, yes, I heard him," John said. "We'll be heading back now. Oh, and thanks for not shooting us on sight."

"That's okay," the guard replied, giving a serious answer to what had been a joking remark.

As they were walking away, Jenny reached down to rub some of the residue off her shoe. Lifting her finger to her nose, she sniffed it, then made a face.

"What is it? What are you doing?"

"I saw some residue on the ground back there and I wanted to check it out, so I rubbed my shoe in it."

"So, what did you find?"

"It's ammonium nitrate, the same ingredient that went into the bomb used to bring down the Murrah Building. And the North Dallas Jewish Children's Center," she added after a short pause.

SIXTEEN

Detroit

Paul had just turned off Van Dyke Lylord when a police car pulled up behind him, lights flashing.

"Shit," Paul said, pulling to the side of the road.

"What's wrong?" Linda asked. "You didn't make an illegal turn."

"I'm a black man driving a classic 'Vette," Paul said. "That fits the profile."

"Profile?"

"The profile says that the only way a black man can afford to drive a car like this is if he is an athlete, in show business, or dealing in drugs."

Linda turned to watch the policemen. One of them said something into the car radio; then both of them got out. However, only one approached Paul's side of the car. The other one stood just behind and to the right of the Corvette, taking up a position of observation at a forty-five-degree angle from the right rear fender.

The approaching policeman hitched up his trousers as he came even with the car, then looked the car over with a long, slow, appreciative stare. He nodded. "This is one good-lookin' car," he said. "Fifty-eight?"

"Close," Paul replied. "Fifty-seven. The fifty-eight had four headlights."

"Right. I should've known that," the policeman said. "Is this your car?"

"Yes, it is."

"How much would a car like this set you back, do you suppose?"

"About forty-five thousand dollars."

The policeman whistled. "That's a year's pay," he said. "That is, it's a year's pay for a working man. Someone like you, it probably doesn't make any difference."

"Someone like me?"

"You may have"—the policeman paused for a moment—"alternative means of income."

"Why did you stop me, Officer?" Paul asked. "If you've got a charge to make, make it."

"Sir, would you show me your driver's license and vehicle registration?" the policeman asked.

"Why do I need to do that?" Paul asked. "I didn't violate any traffic laws."

"From time to time we do a routine license and registration check," the policeman replied.

"Have you checked anyone else today?"

"Your license and registration, please," the policeman repeated.

Linda flashed the policeman her prettiest smile. "Is anything wrong, Officer?"

"Miss, I'm dealing with this gentleman now. If you would, please just sit there and keep your mouth shut."

The smile left Linda's face, to be replaced by a smoldering glare.

Paul showed him his license and the car registration. The policeman examined the papers for a moment, then looked up at Paul again. "Didn't you tell me this was your car?"

"Yes."

"Then you want to explain why your driver's license

is issued to a Paul Clark, but the car is registered to Paul Brewer?"

Paul took in a quick breath. Don Yee had made new driver's licenses and other identity cards for everyone to use while they were undercover. But Paul had forgotten to change his vehicle registration.

"You want to get out of the car?" the policeman said. "You, too, miss."

"Look, I can explain," Paul began, but the policeman pulled his pistol and pointed it at Paul, using the two-handed target-grip.

"I said get out of the car now!" he shouted.

The backup police officer came quickly up the opposite side of the car. "Get out, miss!" he said. Put your hands on the hood of the car!"

Paul and Linda both exited the car as ordered, then, also as ordered, put their hands on the hood of the car, Paul on one side, Linda on the other. With one of the officers keeping them covered, the other began searching. He began with Linda first, and as he moved his hand up the inside of her leg, he put a little too much pressure and lingered a little too long at the junction of her legs.

"Search me, don't feel me up," Linda said pointedly.

"Now, honey, don't tell me you've never had a white man there," the policeman replied. "If you haven't, your mama has. You're damn near as white as I am."

"Keep your mind on business, Culpepper," the other officer ordered.

"She's clean," Culpepper said, stepping back from Linda.

"Now," Paul said quietly.

Without a second's hesitation, Linda struck out with her right leg. Her foot found Culpepper's groin, and with an agonizing groan, he doubled over. Linda spun around then, sending her second kick straight at Culpepper's chin. He went down.

The officer holding the pistol was so surprised by Linda's unexpected action that he let his attention wander. That was all the opening Paul needed. Coming off the hood of the car, Paul used his left hand to grab the policeman's pistol, jerking it away cleanly. A roundhouse blow with his right put this policeman on the ground with the other.

"Get their radios!" Paul shouted. While Linda took their portable radios from them, Paul ran back to the police car. Reaching inside, he popped the videotape from the observation camera, then, stepping back, used the policeman's own gun to fire into the fuel tank. Gasoline began bubbling out through the bullet holes as Paul rushed back to his car. By the time he reached the Corvette, Linda was already hopping into the car with both of the officers' remote radios in her hand.

Paul started the 'Vette, whipping it into a 180-degree turn. By now gasoline had begun to pool under the police car. Stopping alongside the car for a moment, Paul snapped a match head with his thumbnail. With the match ignited, he dropped it into the pool of fuel, then sped away from the scene with his tires squealing in protest. When they were half a block away, the police car exploded into a ball of flame.

Twisting around in her seat, Linda saw the two policemen, on their feet now, watching helplessly as their car burned. She laughed.

"Have a good time, did you?" Paul asked.

"Well, yes, sort of," Linda replied.

"You still don't get it, do you?"

"What?"

"Why we were stopped."

"The profile thing?"

"The profile thing. The only reason they stopped

me was because I was black and I was driving an expensive car."

"Well, when you stop to think about it, it makes sense," Linda said. "At least from a law-enforcement point of view. I mean, you have to face it, Paul. When you see a young black man driving a flashy car, the chances are much more likely that he is a drug-dealer than he is a stockbroker or a doctor."

"Shit, you're as bad as they are."

"I've never made any bones about the way I feel about it," Linda said. "Blacks make up about twelve percent of the population, but they commit nearly fifty percent of the violent crime."

"Did you like the way that cop was talking to you while he was feeling you up?"

Linda was silent for a moment. "No. I wanted to jerk that honky motherfucker's tongue out of his mouth and hand it to him."

Paul burst into howls of laughter. "Honky motherfucker?" he said. He laughed so hard that tears began streaming down his cheeks. "Damn, girl. You might pass as a sister after all."

Fort Freedom

"Whenever possible, we discourage our people from leaving the compound," General Grant said when John and Jenny told him they would like their Jeep back so they could go into nearby Poplar Bluff.

"Why is that?" John asked.

"Security reasons."

"General, surely you don't think either one of us would represent a security risk?" Jenny asked.

"Either of you personally? No," General Grant said, shaking his head. "But you must know that, for all intents and purposes, we are at war. We have been targeted by the FBI, the BAIF, the IRS, and who knows how many other government agencies. Every time any of our people go into town, it increases the risk."

"I can understand that," Jenny said. "But I really need a few things from town."

"Make out a list," General Grant said. "Next time we have an authorized visit to town, I'll see to it that what you want is picked up."

"Thank you," Jenny said. "I will make out a list." She and John started to leave. Then, almost as an afterthought, she turned back. "Oh, and I'm expecting a package to be delivered to me, general delivery, at the Poplar Bluff post office. I didn't know if you had mail delivered out here, and even if you did, I thought it might be better to be a little more circumspect."

General Grant smiled. "That was a good move on your part," he said. "I'm glad to see that you are security-conscious. As a matter of curiosity, what have you ordered?"

"A box of nine-millimeter shells for my Walther P-38."

Grant looked confused. "You didn't have to do that. We do have a well-stocked armory. If you needed a box of ammunition, I'm sure we could have supplied it."

"Not these shells, General. These are very particular shells. They can only be ordered from a special supplier. You see, the P-38 was the side arm of the German officer during World War II. And these particular shells are left over from the preserved inventory that was designated for the Waffen SS. And as everyone knows, only the best equipment was reserved for the SS."

Grant laughed. "Well, who am I to stand in the way of a quest for excellence? I'll see to it that your package is picked up."

"Thank you."

* * *

Chicago

From the moment Carter Phillips put his offer on the Website, it became one of the most popular sites on the net. There were thousands of hits, and well over one hundred offers to buy the nuclear warhead he had acquired. Some of the responses were from Third World nations that sought the weapon to establish dominance in their own sphere. Phillips ruled them out because they were too public and his personal exposure would be too high. He wished he could ask Congressman Anderson who he was supposed to sell the device to, but Anderson was very specific when he explained the concept of a firewall. Phillips couldn't go to Anderson. He was going to have to filter through all the offers, then make his own decision as to who should be his customer.

Phillips knew that most of the offers were bogus, and some were certain to be part of a sting operation. But he was well prepared to sort through all the clutter, whether the offers were bogus or deceptive. In fact, he had decided it was precisely his ability to do this that made him an attractive contact for Anderson. Phillips designed a special screening program that, based upon the responses of those who had tendered an offer, would establish a probability rate. The probability rate measured everything from the prospective client's actual intent to buy, to his financial capability, to the likelihood that he would be the client Otto Maass had spoken of. Only two of the many bidders had survived the screening, and Carter had already opened negotiations with them, suggesting St. Louis as the meeting place. He chose St. Louis for two reasons. It wasn't very far from Chicago, and Carter had absolutely no personal connection to St. Louis.

If everything went as planned, Carter would clear at least two million dollars from this operation. That was nothing compared to his "worth on paper" just a year earlier, when he'd owned two million shares of stock that was selling for $126 per share. Today the stock was worth twenty-two cents per share and his entire operation was in free fall. But two million un-encumbered dollars, as well as personal control of the patent for media-fusion, would make his landing a little softer.

Wiregrass, Alabama

At first glance the picnic thrown by the Alabama Knights of the White Orchid looked like any company, civic group, or church picnic. Someone was barbecu-ing on a grill that was fashioned from a fifty-gallon oil drum, cut lengthwise, then welded to a set of steel legs. The barbecue chef lifted the lid to a cloud of aromatic smoke, then brushed the three glistening pork shoulders with a secret-recipe barbecue sauce. The cook was wearing an apron with the cartoon draw-ing of a pig, standing on its hind legs, wearing an apron and chef's hat as it turned a spit over an open fire. Skewered upon the spit was a caricature of Bill Clinton.

Women were filling the tables with potato salad, coleslaw, baked beans, home-canned pickles, and an assortment of cakes and pies. Children were running about the grounds laughing, while some of the younger men and women were engaged in a spirited game of softball. The difference between this picnic and other picnics was the fact that more than half of the men, and even a large number of women, were wearing pistols, while several men walked around with rifles slung over their shoulders. Dozens of Confederate flags dotted the area, and a hand-painted sign on the road leading into the parking lot read:

White Christians Only
All others will be shot

"Jesus, look at this," Chris said as he and Bob walked from the parking lot toward the picnic area. "It's unreal."

"No, it's very real," Bob replied. "That's the problem."

"Hold it!" an armed man challenged, stepping out from behind a tree and pointing a rifle toward them. "This here is a private picnic."

"It's all right, George," Arnie called from a nearby table. "Let 'em in."

"Okay, if you say so, Arnie," George replied.

Pasting on a grin, Bob started toward Arnie. Arnie was sitting on the table, with his legs on the bench seat.

"You boys grab a beer from that number-two washtub over there, and join me," Arnie said.

Bob nodded, then stuck his hand down into the cold water, pulling up a can of beer that had little pieces of ice clinging to it. The can was so cold that it hurt Bob's hand to hold it, but he pulled open the pop-top, let it spew a bit, then took a drink. Chris did the same thing as he followed Bob over to the table.

"Here, I'll sit on the seat, give you two boys a little bit of room," Arnie said, stepping down from the table.

Arnie sat on one side of the table while Bob and Chris sat on the other.

"Now," Arnie said, taking a beer and wiping the back of his hand across his mouth. He smiled across the table at Bob and Chris. "Just who the fuck are you two yahoos?"

"What?" Bob replied with a little chuckle.

The smile left Arnie's face.

"I did some checkin' up, and found out that nobody down in Baldwin County has ever heard of either one of you," Arnie said.

"Baldwin County is a big county," Bob said. "Fact is, in area, it's the biggest county east of the Mississippi River, did you know that?"

"I ain't interested in any of that chamber of commerce shit," Arnie said. "I told you I did some checking. We ran your fingerprints."

"Fingerprints?"

"Oh, didn't I tell you? I'm a deputy sheriff. Fact is, we got maybe half-a-dozen law-enforcement officers in our little group. It was real easy to lift your fingerprints off the beers you boys drank when you come to our meetin' the other night. We sent 'em in to some friends we got in the FBI, and you'd be surprised at what we found out."

Arnie looked at Bob. "Now, take you, for example. Your real name is Bob Garrett. You are forty-four years old, you spent fifteen years with the National Security Agency, and five years before that with the CIA."

Arnie switched his attention to Chris. "Your real name is Chris Farmer. You are thirty-two, and a former one-time member of the Secret Service. You never played football for Mississippi State. You were a tight end for Missouri University. Missouri, for Chrissake. But that ain't the worst part. No, sir, the worst part is you actually used to protect Bill Clinton. And as far as I'm concerned, anyone who would protect that traitor is a traitor hisself."

Almost casually, Arnie raised his hand. When he did so, half-a-dozen armed men came toward them.

Bob started to get up, but one of the armed men hit him between the shoulders with the butt of his rifle. The pain rushed from the point of impact up to his neck, then down his back all the way to his knees, then circled around into his abdomen. It was so severe that, for a moment, he was afraid he might throw up.

"Hurts, don't it?" Arnie asked casually. He took another swallow of his beer. "Now, sit your ass down, boy."

Bob did as he was instructed.

"What now?" Chris asked.

"Now that's a good question," Arnie said. "What now? I don't want to kill you two here, at the picnic. It might upset the chil'run and a few of the more squeamish womenfolk."

"Yeah, I'd be a little squeamish about that myself," Chris said.

Arnie laughed. "You got a good sense of humor, boy. I like that in a fella," he said.

"So, you're going to let us go and tell us not to do it again?" Bob asked.

"You two boys kill me, you know that? Well, actually that's wrong. I'm going to kill you." Arnie laughed again. "You kill me, no, I'm going to kill you. That's a good one, you get it?"

"Yeah, we get it," Bob said. "But what about the kids and the squeamish ladies?"

"Well, I've figured out how I'm going to handle that. I aim to have a trial, right here, right now. We'll try you two boys, find your asses guilty, and sentence you to die. That way the chil'run can see what happens to traitors, but they won't actually have to watch the sentence being carried out. Cuff 'em," he said, and Bob and Chris had their arms pulled behind their backs while handcuffs were put on their wrists.

"Where is this trial to be held?" Chris asked.

"Why, right here," Arnie replied. "Every good picnic has to have some kind of entertainment. You boys are goin' to provide that for us."

SEVENTEEN

True to his promise, Arnie Stone, as Grand Google of the Alabama Knights of the White Orchid, convened a court hearing right there in the park. The scene was surreal, with birds singing in the trees and children playing and laughing nearby. Out on the blacktop state highway, cars and trucks passed by, their drivers and passengers blissfully unaware of what was going on in this pastoral setting alongside the road.

Nearly a hundred men and women, members of the Wiregrass chapter, were sitting in the gallery, making use of folding chairs, picnic coolers, or blankets spread on the ground. Arnie was the judge, and Frank Norton was the prosecutor, while the jury was composed of a panel of men and women selected from the group.

"Laurabelle, will you see to my baked beans?" one woman asked as she took off her apron and started toward the two rows of folding chairs that had been put out for the jury. "I've got a Styrofoam container for 'em. That'll keep 'em warm till all this is done."

"Sure thing, Mae," Laurabelle replied. "You just go ahead and do your duty. I'll tend to things."

Mae took her seat with the rest of the jury. The jury was composed of nine men and three women.

"As you can see," Arnie said to Bob and Chris while pointing to the jury, "we got us a jury and a prosecutor. So, before we hang you traitorous sonofabitchin' government assholes, we aim to give you a fair trail."

"We have no defense attorney?" Bob asked.

Arnie smiled. "I'd be real pleased to appoint one for you," he said. "But there prob'ly ain't a man or woman here who don't want to see you shot. So in the interest of fairness, I figured you'd just as soon act as your own attorneys."

"You've got that right," Bob said.

"Will you at least remove our handcuffs during the trial?" Chris asked.

Arnie glanced over at Frank Norton, who had pulled a chair up behind a card table and was now busily writing on a yellow tablet.

"Does prosecution have any objection to removing the handcuffs during the trial?"

Frank looked up from his tablet. "No objections, Your Honor."

"Billy, take the cuffs off, but keep a close eye on 'em," Arnie ordered.

"Sure thing, Arnie," Billy replied.

Arnie, who had appropriated a picnic table for his bench, hit the table with the hammer he was using as a gavel. "Billy, the court hereby fines you twenty-five dollars for contempt."

"What?" Billy asked in surprise. "What the hell did I do?"

"Fifty dollars," Arnie said.

"Fifty dollars? Goddamnit, Arnie, you can't just keep finin' me without tellin' me what it is I'm a-doin' that's causing you to fine me."

"I will be addressed as Your Honor," Arnie said.

"Oh, sorry 'bout that, Your Honor," Billy said contritely. He unlocked the handcuffs, and Chris and Bob rubbed their wrists gingerly.

"Well, if you're sorry, the fine is suspended," Arnie

said. He looked over at Frank. "Is prosecution ready to begin?"

Frank stood up. "I'm ready, Your Honor."

"You may make your opening statement."

Frank walked over to stand in front of the jury. For a moment or two he just stood there, looking at them, staring into the face of each of them. Then he pointed toward Bob and Chris.

"Them two boys over there is government agents. The both of 'em," he said. "The one on the right is Bob Garrett.

"Mr. Garrett started his career with the CIA. No tellin' what kind of evil he did while he was with them. From there, he moved to the National Security Agency. After that, we lose track of him, which means he's gone undercover.

"Now, why would he go undercover? Well, maybe so he could pretend that he is someone he ain't, and he could join up with a group of patriotic white Christian men and women like, oh, maybe the Alabama Knights of the White Orchid. Now, why would he want to join us? So he could be a viper in our midst, a traitor who would bring the federal government down on us just like they come down on Ruby Ridge, Waco, and Sky Meadow."

Frank paused while he let his words sink in. Then he walked over to stand in front of the two defendants. There, he pointed to Chris.

"Now, what about the big man here, the former football player? What is his background?

"Well, for one thing, he didn't play for Mississippi State like he told us he did. He played for Missouri. But when you think about it, that ain't nothin' to get all pissed off about. I mean, hell, if playin' for Missouri is the best you can do, why, I reckon I would lie, too."

The jury and the gallery laughed.

"No, ladies and gentlemen of the jury. The sin Mr.

Chris Farmer committed was to be a member of the Secret Service. Now, do you know what the Secret Service does? They guard the President."

He spun back toward Chris, then pointed an accusing finger at him.

"There's not a doubt in my mind but that this sonofabitch stood guard outside the Oval Office door while our former President was getting hisself serviced by, hell, no tellin' how many young girls. I wouldn't be surprised if he didn't pimp for the President."

The reaction of disapproval was immediate and loud, and Arnie had to pound his hammer on the table to quiet them.

"You've got to excuse the jury and these fine folks, Your Honor," Frank said. He looked toward Bob and Chris, his mouth curling into a snarl. "Any decent white man or woman couldn't help but be disgusted with these two traitors to our race. They're guilty as hell, both of 'em, and I rest my case."

Arnie slammed his hammer onto the table, then looked over at the two defendants. "The court finds you both guilty. Have either of you got anything to say in your defense?"

"Wait a minute," Bob said. "You find us guilty; *then* you tell us we can say something in our defense?"

Arnie smiled. "It makes for a more efficient court," he said.

"What was the purpose of the jury, if you are going to find us guilty?"

Arnie looked over toward the jury. "Any of you disagree with my finding?" he asked.

No one spoke.

"Looks like the jury concurs," Arnie said.

"Your Honor, let me take 'em both off somewhere and take care of 'em," Frank said.

"I ain't passed sentence yet," Arnie said. "Fact is,

as the prosecutor, you ain't even asked for a sentence."

"There ain't but one penalty for spies," Frank said. "And that's to take them out and shoot them. As prosecutor, I would like to claim that right."

Arnie stroked his chin for a moment as if considering Frank's request. Then he nodded. "All right," he said. "But take 'em somewhere else to do it. I'd just as soon not spoil our picnic. And I for sure don't want 'em traced back to us."

"I'll take care of 'em," Frank said.

"Go with 'im, Billy," Arnie ordered.

"No need for that, Your Honor," Frank said. "The fewer people that get involved in this, the better it'll be."

Arnie laughed cynically. "You think everyone here ain't involved?" he asked. "In this case, the more folks there are involved, the better it is. We sort of have a mutual-protection society that way. Go with 'em, Billy."

"Okay, Ar . . . uh, Your Honor," Billy said.

"Don't have to say Your Honor now," Arnie said. "I done adjourned court."

Billy put the handcuffs back on Chris and Bob, then looked toward Frank. "What now?"

"We'll walk 'em over to the parking lot," Frank said. "Then take 'em in their own truck. That way, when the bodies are found, they won't be able to trace 'em back to us through any vehicle. Johnny, let me have your rifle."

Johnny, who was holding an AK-47, handed it over. "Don't forget where you got that," he said.

"Don't worry," Frank replied. He jabbed the barrel of the rifle painfully into Bob's back. "Okay, boys, let's go."

Frank and Billy started walking Bob and Chris across a wide expanse of grass, toward the parking lot, some one hundred yards away from where the trial had taken place.

"All right folks, the show's over," Arnie said to the others as the little group marched away. "What do you say we sit down to lunch now? All this has made me hungry."

"Laurabelle, did you take care of my beans?" Mae asked as she picked her way out of the two rows of chairs where the jury had sat.

"I sure did, hon. They're just fine, I know they are," Laurabelle answered.

"How we all going to ride in that truck?" Billy asked as they approached the parking lot. "We can't all sit in the front seat. And who's going to drive?"

"I'll drive," Frank said. "We'll put the prisoners in the back, and you can ride back there with them, keeping an eye on them."

"I hope you ain't plannin' on going through any towns or anything," Billy said.

"Yeah, you've got a point," Frank said. "Better take their handcuffs off. That way it won't look as suspicious."

Billy nodded, then unlocked the handcuffs. Again, Bob and Chris rubbed their wrists.

"They always do that," Billy said, pointing at them and laughing. "Them things hurt, do they?"

"Billy?" Frank said.

"Yeah?" Billy looked toward Frank. As he did, Frank brought the butt of the rifle up hard in a vertical butt-stroke. Billy went down.

Bob and Chris looked at Frank with an expression of shock on their faces.

"Ira Preston, FBI," Frank said. "You've just caused me to blow my cover, but I couldn't let you be killed. Get in the truck, fast."

"Damn!" Chris said. "Are you a pleasant surprise!"

"Uh-oh," Bob said. "They must've seen you take out Billy. Look!"

Looking back toward the picnic area, the three men saw several of the White Orchids running across the field toward them. Two of the pursuers raised rifles and fired. Bob saw puffs of smoke coming from the ends of the barrels of the rifles, even as he heard the bullets whiz angrily by his ear.

"Let's go!" Bob said. The three had started toward the pickup when Bob suddenly stopped in his tracks. "Shit!" he shouted. "They took my keys!"

That had happened earlier when Bob and Chris were placed in handcuffs. Arnie had relieved them of their billfolds, keys, and all other possessions.

"We'll have to go in your vehicle!" Chris said to Frank/Ira.

"I didn't bring one," Ira said. "I rode out here with Arnie."

By now the bullets were flying by like angry bees, and the men could hear them hitting the ground around them, or slamming into the cars and trucks in the parking lot behind them.

"Get in, I'll jump the ignition!" Bob said as he hurried around to the driver's side of the truck.

"Be quick about it!" Ira said. "I'll hold them off as long as I can!"

Ira turned the AK-47 toward the men who were charging across the field. Although the AK-47 had been modified to allow it to fire in the fully automatic mode, to do so would expend the ammunition too quickly. Therefore Ira squeezed his rounds off one at a time, though he did that rather rapidly, firing as fast as he could pull the trigger.

Reaching under the dash, Bob crossed the ignition wires, then was gratified to hear the starter turn. A second later the engine kicked off with a roar through the glass-pack mufflers.

"Get in!" Bob shouted to Ira. Chris was already in the truck.

Still firing, Ira started backing toward the truck. Finally he reached it, then stepped up through the open door.

"Damn!" Ira said, smiling from ear to ear. "Haven't had this much fun since Granny got her tit caught in the food processor. Let's get the hell out of . . ."

Ira was unable to finish his sentence because a bullet caught him in the back of the neck. His eyes rolled up in his head, and he fell back off the truck.

"Ira!" Chris shouted, reaching for him. He wasn't able to prevent him from falling all the way to the ground. Chris started to get out of the truck to get him, even as bullets began slamming through the cab of the truck.

"Leave him!" Bob called. "He's dead!"

Bob shoved the accelerator to the floor, and the souped-up engine responded. He whipped the truck into a 180-degree turn, with the spinning wheels throwing back mud and gravel. He started through the parking lot toward the entrance, only to see that another pickup truck had been brought up to block the way. This was the truck that had been used to haul some material out onto the picnic area, so it hadn't been in the parking lot. As a result, it was immediately available to come up fast, and some of the pursuers were taking advantage of it. Three armed men were in the back of the truck, firing at Bob and Chris as they tried to leave the parking lot.

"Can't go that way," Chris shouted.

"Hang on!" Bob replied.

Turning hard to the right, Bob drove to the end of the parking lot, crashed through the low-rail fence that surrounded the lot, then started out across a wide, grassy flat. At the other end of the flat was a gently rising hill. The incline was too high to see what was beyond it. Pushing the accelerator all the way to the floor, Bob headed right for the incline. The speedometer needle quivered at eighty miles per hour on a gauge that only registered to eighty-five.

"Jesus, Bob, what are you doing?"

"I'm going to fly off the top of that hill up there," Bob said.

"What the hell is on the other side?" Chris asked.

"I have no idea," Bob replied. He chuckled. "Wish I had had time to put on the seat belt."

Chris reached across Bob, pulled the seat belt down, and fastened it for him. He managed to get his own seat belt fastened just as they started up.

"Oh, shit!" Chris yelled, bracing himself as much as possible.

Bob gripped the steering wheel hard. He glanced at the speedometer just as they started up the incline, and saw that the needle had buried itself. As the truck started up the hill the windshield was filled with nothing but sky. He had no idea what he would see when he reached the top.

The truck flew over the other side, giving Bob and Chris a sickening moment of weightlessness. Below them was the same blacktop farm-to-market road that passed by the picnic grounds. Coming up the road at that precise moment was a car, followed by an eighteen-wheeler fuel-tank truck. Incredibly, the pickup flew over the top of the car, just as stunt drivers' cars do in thrill shows, using ramps to jump over long lines of cars or school buses.

The reason for the incline was because at this particular point, the farm-to-market road was running through a cut. Bob's pickup truck flew across the road, and over the car, then landed on the grassy knoll on the other side. Although both Bob and Chris were

jarred from head to toe by the impact, the truck survived the landing.

Behind them, the pickup truck that was in pursuit
tried to make the same jump. As it flew over the incline, then started across, the three men who were
riding in the bed of the truck were thrown clear. This
driver wasn't as lucky as Bob had been, because his
truck lacked the momentum needed to carry him all
the way across. The timing couldn't have been worse,
because this was the precise moment of the arrival of
the eighteen-wheeler tanker truck. The pickup
slammed into the side of the trailer of the tanker
truck. The collision was followed a second later by a
huge fireball.

Bob had stood on the brakes almost as soon as his
truck hit the ground on the other side. The truck went
into a long, spinning slide on the grass, skidding
around so that though the momentum was still taking
them away from the highway, they were actually looking back toward it as the pursuing pickup slammed
into the side of the gasoline tanker. They had a very
close view of the explosion.

Finally, the skidding came to a halt, and they found
themselves sitting in the truck, nearly fifty yards away
from the highway, while shrapnel from the explosion
rained down all around them. Miraculously, none of
the debris hit them, though there were several flaming
pieces on the ground all around.

"You all right?" Bob asked.

"Yeah," Chris answered. "Will this thing still run?"

"I think so."

"What do you say we get the hell out of here?"

Bob drove back up onto the highway, then started
north, leaving the conflagration behind. They were
nearly ten miles away before they saw the first emergency vehicles heading toward the scene.

EIGHTEEN

Detroit

"The first thing you're going to have to do is get rid of that car," Kwazi said.

"The hell you say. I'm not getting rid of my 'Vette."

"You've got no choice. You'll have every cop in Michigan looking for it. And let's face it, it's not a car that blends into the background."

"I'll take my chances."

Kwazi laughed. "Still, that must've been some sight to see, the cops standing there watching their car burn."

News of the confrontation involving Paul, Linda, and the police had reached the headquarters of the Oppressed Brotherhood even before Paul and Linda returned. It was on all the TV stations, with pictures of the police car in flames and the two embarrassed and enraged policemen standing alongside. The perpetrators were described as a "powerfully built African American man, accompanied by a light-skinned, very attractive African American female. They are driving a 1957 Corvette, black, with red coves." The reporter had had to explain that "coves" meant the scoops behind the front wheels.

"We'll find a place to hide your car," Kwazi promised. "In the meantime, I want you two to be prepared to take a trip with me."

"Where are we going?"

"St. Louis."

"What's in St. Louis?" Linda asked.

"Girl, first thing you have to learn as my bodyguard is, don't ask so many questions."

"Sorry."

Kwazi smiled. "I'll tell you this, though. If the St. Louis trip works out the way I think it will, the Oppressed Brotherhood will be oppressed no longer."

"Kwazi," Ibo Mogombi said, sticking his head in through the door. "Mooli Nyumbui is here."

Kwazi smiled broadly. "Send Brother Nyumbui in," he said. He looked over at Paul and Linda. "I've been wanting you to meet Nyumbui," he said. "He's been with me longer than anyone." More quietly he added, "He was actually one of my students back at Stanford, so he is one of the few people who knows all about me."

"Kwazi," a deep voice said then, Nyumbui coming into the room to greet him. The new arrival was a powerfully built man with broad shoulders and a trim belly. He was obviously someone who took pride in his appearance and worked hard to stay in condition. A bit of gray at his temples put his age as late forties to early fifties. The two men greeted each other with the closed-fist "dap." Then Kwazi turned toward Paul and Linda.

"Mooli, I want you to meet my new bodyguards, Paul Clark and his lady friend, Linda."

Nyumbui looked toward the two. When he saw Linda, he smiled broadly. "Well, now, my man, I've got to tell you, you have one fine-looking bodyguard." He looked toward Paul, frowned, then looked back at Kwazi. "Who'd you say this is?"

"Paul Clark," Kwazi said.

"The hell it is. I done butted heads too many times with this motherfucker up in the CFL to know better than that. This is Paul Brewer."

"Keith Chambers," Paul said easily. "How are you doing these days? I sort of lost track of you once you retired from football."

"I was right. You are Paul Brewer, aren't you?"

"Yes."

"What'd you change your name for?" Keith asked.

Paul laughed. "Why you asking me that, my man? What do you mean why did I change my name? I just changed part of it. What name are you going by now? Mooli Nyumbui? That's a hell of a lot more change than I did."

"Ain't the same thing, man, and you know it," Mooli said. "All I did was get rid of my slave name. You . . ." Keith stopped in mid-sentence. Then his face grew very hard. "Wait a minute, motherfucker! I know what happened to you now! You went to work for the fuckin' government."

Linda looked shocked and stepped away from Paul, moving closer to Kwazi.

"Is what he's saying true?" she asked Paul. "You're with the government?"

"I was. I'm no longer with them," Paul said.

"Yeah? Well, let me tell you somethin', baby, you no longer with me either," Linda said. "Far as I'm concerned, once a pig, always a pig."

"Yeah, sweet thing, you get over here with me," Kwazi said.

"You damn right I'm going to get next to you," Linda said. "I don't want nothin' to do with that pig. Huh-uh, baby."

"Linda, you know me better than that," Paul pleaded. "Come on, how long we been together? I ever done anything make you think I'm still a cop?"

By now, Linda was standing right beside Kwazi, glaring at Paul.

"Brother Man Brewer, looks like your luck just run out," Mooli said, smiling at Paul.

"Only thing left now is to try and figure out what to do with you," Kawzi said. "Maybe I—" Before Kwazi could finish his sentence, Linda suddenly stepped behind him and crossed her arms around his neck, putting pressure against it.

"What the hell?" Kwazi asked, his voice restricted by Linda's arm lock. "What the fuck you doin', girl?" Kwazi tried to struggle, but Linda increased the pressure on his neck.

"I wouldn't struggle if I were you," Linda said calmly. "All it takes from me is a little pressure, and you'll wind up in a wheelchair for life, just like Superman. Mr. Chambers, I'm sure you are armed. I'd like you to take your gun out, using only your thumb and forefinger please, and put it gently on the floor."

"Say what?" Mooli asked. "You fuckin' crazy, or what? I ain't goin' to take my gun out just 'cause you got your scrawny-assed little arm around his neck."

Kwazi's eyes were wide with fear. "Do what she says, Mooli. Believe me, the bitch can do it," Kwazi said, his voice quivering.

"Better listen to the man, Chambers," Paul said.

"What if I don't?"

"If you don't, two things will happen," Paul replied, pulling his pistol. "Kwazi will be paralyzed for life, and I'll come through you like shit through a goose. Pretty much the way I used to come through you when you were a burned-out has-been tackle in the CFL."

With Mooli now covered, Linda let go of Kwazi and walked over to relieve Mooli of his gun. Then Paul indicated with a wave of his pistol that the two men should move over to stand by the radiator. It took less than a minute for Linda to secure both of them by the simple but very effective procedure of having them put their hands behind their back, one on each side of the radiator pipe, then tying their thumbs together with shoestring. She followed that by gagging them with their own socks.

"Ohh, man, this is ripe," Linda said, wrinkling her nose as she began stuffing Mooli's socks into his mouth. "I guess this'll teach you to wash your feet more often."

"Get rid of whoever is out front," Paul told Linda.

Nodding, Linda stepped through the door out into the large, open room that was the headquarters of the Oppressed Brotherhood. Ibo was sitting in a chair, tipped back against the wall, looking at a magazine. At the moment, he had the magazine held up and turned sideways to better enjoy the centerfold.

"Ibo," Linda said flirtatiously. "What are you doing? Looking at centerfold models? I'm hurt. I thought I was the only one for you."

"What?" Ibo said, surprised by her comment. "What you talkin' 'bout, girl? You be Paul's woman."

"Well, that's true," Linda said. She looked back toward the door she had just come through. "Most of the time," she added seductively. She put her fingers on Ibo's cheek.

"Look here, girl. What's goin' on?" Ibo asked.

"Paul is in there with Kwazi and Mooli. Turns out Paul and Mooli played football together up in Canada, and now they're having an old-timers' reunion."

"Really? They played football together?" Ibo asked, standing up and looking toward the door. "Damn, I'd like to listen in on that conversation."

"Oh?" Linda said, pouting. "Well, then, I guess I'll just have to find someone else."

"Find someone else for what?" Ibo asked.

"For a little . . . sport fucking," Linda said, running the tips of her fingers across Ibo's lips. "You do recognize fucking as a sport, don't you?"

Nervously, Ibo looked toward the door again.

"Oh, don't worry about Paul. I've done this before. Paul never has to find out about it. I know how to keep a secret. The question is, can you?"

"Yeah," Ibo said, breathing heavily now. "Yeah, I can keep a secret."

"Good. You know that motel down the street a couple of blocks? The one called Cloud Nine?"

"Yeah, I know it."

Linda leaned over to whisper to him, her breath caressing his cheek, her tongue flipping lightly against his earlobe.

"Get a room there, baby," she said in a husky voice. "I'll be down there in five minutes."

"Yeah," Ibo said anxiously, starting toward the front door. "Cloud Nine. Okay, I'll . . . wait. Pig Meat and Dooley are gone. I was supposed to watch things till they get back."

"Believe me, Kwazi and Mooli are tied up in there. They'll never know you're gone." She smiled. "Besides, I don't know about you, but when I get in the mood like this, it never takes me very long."

"Ha! It won't take me no time at all!" Ibo said. "Why, I can get off in about a minute!"

"What a man," Linda said, wrapping her arms around herself and wriggling her body provocatively. "I'm getting hot just thinking about it. Hurry!"

"I'm hurrying!" Ibo said, dashing through the front door.

Linda stepped up to the big picture window in front of the old converted store to watch Ibo run down the street. She waited until he turned into the motel parking lot; then she returned to the back room.

"It's all clear," she said. "Let's get out of here."

"Where's Ibo?" Paul asked.

"He's hurrying to keep an appointment."

"Okay, let's go."

Paul and Linda started to leave, but as they started through the door, Paul turned back toward Kwazi and Mooli, both of whom were still bound and gagged. They stared back at him, the hate in their eyes palpable. "Nice running into you again, Keith," Paul said.

Mooli grunted something, but he couldn't be heard through the gag. His temple was throbbing in anger. Paul and Linda hurried out front, climbed into the 'Vette, then drove away. As they drove by the Cloud Nine Motel, Linda laughed out loud.

"What is it?" Paul asked.

"I'm just wondering if Ibo is up for his appointment."

Paul shook his head. "My pappy said I'd never be able to understand women, and he was right."

Inside Room 115, Ibo lay on the bed on top of the covers. He was totally naked and, because he was anticipating the arrival of a beautiful woman, fully erect.

"She wants it fast, I'll show the bitch fast," he said aloud. He grabbed himself. "Hell, it won't even take me a minute I'll be so . . . uhnnn . . . uhnn, oh shit!"

In shame, frustration, and embarrassment, Ibo reached for the towel beside the bed.

Fort Freedom

John stood at the window of the cabin that was his quarters and looked out onto the quadrangle. It was ten P.M. and he watched as a bugler approached a megaphone in the middle of the parade ground. The bugler positioned the megaphone, raised the bugle to his lips, and began blowing Taps.

"Can you believe this?" John asked Jenny, who was in the room behind him, sitting at the table. "Grant really does have a militaristic complex, doesn't he? Bugle calls all day, from Reveille to Chow Call to Taps."

They had by now disabled all the listening devices in John's quarters, and were able to speak freely.

"There's something to be said for military discipline," Jenny replied. She dumped the box of nine-millimeter shells onto the table in front of her, then started going through the cartridges one at a time. These were the shells General Grant's courier had picked up for her at the post office's general delivery in Poplar Bluff, Missouri.

Chuckling, John turned away from the window. "Damned if I don't think you could buy into this."

"Well, I'm not for overthrowing the government, if that's what you mean," Jenny said. "But I wouldn't mind being a benevolent dictator for about a month. I'll tell you one damn thing. I could sure as hell clean the country up."

"Benevolent dictator?"

"Yes, benevolent. I would be a gracious leader," Jenny teased.

"You're as full of shit as a Christmas turkey," John said, laughing.

"Ah, here it is," Jenny said, setting one of the cartridges aside. Although not readily apparent, the slug had an X scratched on the nose of the bullet. She began pulling the slug from the casing. Once the slug was separated from the cartridge, she used a pair of tweezers to extract a tiny computer chip. The chip, which was about half the size of a small paper clip, was handed to John. John opened his laptop, then inserted the chip in one of the slots.

"Time to get in touch with Don," he said as he began tapping on the keyboard.

General Grant had established a strict prohibition

against anyone having a cell phone or private access to the Internet. When Felix Coker examined John's computer, one of the things he looked for was anything that would allow John to use the computer as a device for wireless connection. John's laptop passed Coker's initial examination, but now, with the addition of the tiny microchip that had been smuggled in via the shell casing, John was connected.

He began to type.

Code Name Team Headquarters

Lana was watching the various screens and monitors in the communications room. Don was in the kitchen putting the finishing touches on an enormous banana split.

"You sure you don't want me to make one for you?" Don called back to Lana. "It wouldn't be any trouble. I've got everything out."

"One? That thing you are making is only one?" Lana teased.

"Sure, it's only one. What do you think?"

"By my estimate you have used at least a quart of ice cream in its construction."

"Well, the first thing about making a good banana split is not to be skimpy on the base ingredient," Don said as he came back into the communications room. He spooned a generous bite into his mouth. "And as everyone knows, the basic ingredient of a banana split is ice cream."

Laughing, Lana glanced back at the screen. That was when she saw the incoming message.

"Don, it looks like Eagle is trying to make contact with us."

"That would be John," Don said, sitting down at

the keyboard. He put his banana split to one side and began typing:

NEST: Authenticate your transmission, Eagle.
EAGLE: I authenticate Juliet Juliet Bravo Bravo five one five.
NEST: I authenticate Delta Yankee five one five.
EAGLE: Are you paying attention? Or are you eating?
NEST: I'm eating and paying attention. You do want me to keep my strength up, don't you?
EAGLE: Nest, we've had a reference to Gateway. Does that mean anything to you?
NEST: FALCON mentioned Gateway as well, and it has been prominent in e-mail traffic between OB, FN, and Gideon. Have you heard any reference to YELLOWSPARK?
EAGLE: Negative on YELLOWSPARK. But if OB mentioned Gateway, then there has to be some connection.
NEST: Yes, I think so as well. Both OB and FN have been active participants in the on-line bidding. From the increased e-mail traffic, I believe there may be a meeting soon. Perhaps they are going to meet in Gateway to finalize the deal.
EAGLE: I'll see what we can find out.

Fort Freedom

John shut down the computer, then looked over at Jenny, who was just putting away her lab equipment. "You remember when General Grant mentioned St. Louis?"

"Yes, I remember."

"There must be something to it. Paul and Linda

reported that Oppressed Brotherhood was also talking about Gateway."

"Gateway?"

"It's our code for St. Louis. We figured it would be better to be somewhat circumspect when we are establishing contact. I don't think anyone can tap into our transmissions, but you can never be too careful."

"Right. And of course, no one would ever connect Gateway with St. Louis. I mean, what with it being the Gateway to the West and everything," Jenny teased.

John and Don Yee were right to be worried about possible intercepts of their transmissions. Don was good, but so was Felix Coker. Coker had not only bugged all the cabins and rooms, he had also installed radio signal sweeps that would allow him to intercept incoming and outgoing transmissions of all kinds, to include wireless phone and Internet transmissions. As soon as his devices picked up the Internet carrier wave, he was able to feed it into his computer. As a result, the entire exchange between Nest and Eagle was displayed on Felix's monitor.

He logged the entire exchange, then picked up the phone and called General Grant's quarters.

"General Grant," Grant said, answering the phone.

"General, this is Coker. I think maybe you had better get over here to the communications center, sir. There's something you are going to want to see."

"I'll be right there," Grant replied, not wasting time with questions.

It took Grant less than half a minute to cover the distance from his quarters to the communications shack. He saw Coker staring at an array of monitors.

"What is it?" Grant asked.

"I picked up this transmission a few minutes ago," Coker said. "I logged the entire exchange."

Grant read the exchange. "We've got a mole," he said.

"Yes, sir."

"Do you have any idea who it is?"

"It's coming from John Barrone's cabin," Felix said.

"How is he able to do that? I thought you checked out his computer."

"I did. It was clean when I checked it. Somehow, he must've smuggled in a chip."

"Damn," Grant said. "And I would have trusted him with my life." He sighed. "All right, call out the men."

Back in the cabin, John was just closing up the laptop when Jenny happened to look out the window. "Uh-oh," she said.

"What is it?"

"We've got company, and I don't think they are coming for dinner."

"Let's get out of here."

"Wait," Jenny said. "I've got to pick something up in my cabin."

"Damn, just like a woman," John teased. "Always wanting to pick up one last thing."

"You'll want this, I'm sure," she said. "It's a radio-transmitter. Over the last couple of days I've planted a few surprises for them."

"Really? You've been a busy girl. Remind me to be a little nicer to you from now on." They hurried to the window that was on the side of the cabin next to Jenny's cabin. Not only was this window the most convenient to her cabin, it also had the advantage of being blocked off from view by the large bulletin board that had been erected up front, in the space between the two buildings. It was on this bulletin board that General Grant posted his daily orders.

Using the bulletin board as cover, John and Jenny were able to sneak out through the window. They managed to cross over to her quarters without being seen by those who were, slowly but surely, closing in on John's cabin from the front.

John waited outside Jenny's quarters while she wriggled in through her window, retrieved the transmitter, then wriggled back out. She started toward the back of the cabins.

"No, wait," John called out to her. He pointed under the cabin. "We'll crawl out this way. They won't be looking for us under the cabins."

"Good idea," Jenny agreed. Dropping down on her stomach, she slipped under the cabin. John followed close behind.

The dirt under the cabin was dank and foul-smelling, but as John had predicted, it offered them a concealed exit.

Suddenly Jenny froze. "Shit!" she whispered harshly.

"What is it?"

"There's a whole nest of fucking copperhead snakes under here."

"Don't piss 'em off," John said.

"What are you saying? That I'm supposed to get friendly with a snake? What if they don't like me?"

"Ah, don't worry. If one of them bites you, I'll suck the poison out for you. I might even enjoy it. Besides, I'm sure you'd do the same for me."

"Ha, ha," Jenny said sarcastically. "If you want me to suck the poison, then all I can say is you better hope the snake is selective about where he bites."

With a wary eye on the snakes, Jenny and John continued crawling under the cabin until they came to the other side. There, their way was blocked by a latticework trellis that stretched from the base of the wall to the ground. By looking through the latticework, they could see that there was an open space of about fifty yards that would have to be covered between the cabin and their Jeep. Jenny pulled back her hand to smash through the trellis.

"No, wait!" John hissed. "That will make too much noise. Let me help."

Together, they pushed the trellis down, doing it as quietly as they could.

"Okay, let's go," John said, rolling out from under the building.

There were no lights here, but the moon was so bright that it was almost like daylight. They lay on the ground for a moment, assessing the situation.

"Well, now is as good a time as any, I suppose," John said, starting to get up.

"Wait," Jenny said, reaching up to pull him back down.

"Wait on what?"

"A little diversion." Smiling, Jenny raised up on her elbows and pointed her remote device toward a distant pickup truck. She depressed the button and, a second later, the truck exploded with a roar.

"Holy shit!" they heard Keefer shout. "What was that?"

"There! Over there!" someone yelled, and he began firing toward the truck, which was on the opposite side of the parking lot from John and Jenny. As soon as he started firing, the others joined in as well, so that the camp and the surrounding hills were echoing and re-echoing with gunfire.

"Okay, let's go!" John called, getting to his feet while everyone was shooting in the opposite direction. That, of course, was exactly what Jenny had planned, and using the diversion she had caused, they dashed across the open area.

As the group of Freedom Nation soldiers continued to pour fire toward the burning pickup truck, tracer rounds flashed toward the truck, then carried off into the woods, streaking through the darkness.

One of the first things General Grant had done when John and Jenny arrived was take the Jeep keys from them. Those keys were now hanging on a hook just inside the camp headquarters building, along with the keys of all the other vehicles. Grant had explained that it was a matter of security. But John saw it for what it actually was. It was the ultimate means of control, for whoever had the keys had a means of controlling who could and who could not leave the compound.

The loss of the Jeep keys didn't present any real problem to John and Jenny, though. In anticipation of such a thing, John had installed an ignition toggle switch just inside the right front wheel well. Jumping behind the steering wheel, John pushed in the clutch, then nodded at Jenny. Jenny activated the switch and the engine started. She hopped into the passenger's seat, and John put the Jeep in gear and began driving away. They were near the exit drive of the parking lot before Keefer happened to notice them.

"Damn!" he shouted, pointing to the Jeep. "There they are!"

Grant's men swung their weapons around, bringing them to bear on the racing Jeep.

"Holy shit! All hell is about to break loose!" John shouted. "You better do something!"

Jenny turned around and, kneeling in her seat, facing the back, she cut loose with a burst of fire from her P-38 back toward their pursuers. Grant's men had not expected to encounter return fire, and they dropped to the ground in surprise when she opened up on them. Keefer went down, too, but not of his own volition. He had been her initial target, and he was hit by Jenny's deadly accurate fire.

"Son of a bitch! They got Keefer!" someone yelled.

"Stop them!" General Grant ordered. "Sergeant Major Clay! Go after them! Kill them!"

Nodding, Clay started up the side of the hill that flanked the compound.

Jenny pointed the little palm-held transmitter toward the headquarters building. A flick of the switch sent the building up with a roar.

"Ha!" John said. "They'll play hell getting their keys out of there!"

"Some of them won't need to be worrying about keys," Jenny replied. She punctuated her comment by bringing about the remote detonation of at least three more bombs, these, like the first one, planted in vehicles. By the time they were clear of the Fort Freedom compound area, the night was glowing orange from the flickering fire of four pickup trucks and the raging blaze of the headquarters building.

John drove down the narrow dirt road that was the only way into the camp. "Be ready," he cautioned. "The guards will be waiting for us."

"I'm already ready," Jenny replied. "I have a few more surprises in store for them as well."

The guards were waiting at the choke in the road, intending to stop John and Jenny the same way they did the first time, by releasing the spike-studded log and allowing it to swing down across the road. However, just before they could activate the triggering mechanism, Jenny beat them to the punch. She activated two more explosions.

Yesterday, Jenny had planted explosive charges in the very tree that provided the support for the drop-logs. As a result the tree, with the logs attached, came crashing down on the screaming guards. With the final opposition eliminated, the Jeep was able to dart through the last barrier.

"Damn, am I glad to be out of there!" Jenny said in exultation.

"Don't write Grant off yet," John replied. "I don't see us getting away that easily."

"What can he do to us now?"

They were almost all the way to the junction of the dirt road and Highway 60, when Jenny's question was answered. A bullet crashed through the windshield. It had come from somewhere to the left front of the Jeep and, had they not hit a bump at the precise moment the bullet arrived, it would have struck John in the head. Only the fact that his head had jerked to one side involuntarily at the bump had prevented him from being killed.

"Holy shit! Where did that come from?" Jenny asked.

"My guess would be that it is Sergeant Major Clay."

"He's shooting at us in the dark? How can he get so close shooting in the dark?"

"Trust me, dark doesn't mean anything to him. He has a nightscope, and I've seen him shoot before. On the darkest night, he could take out a dime from three hundred yards."

The next shot hit the left front tire and as the tire blew, the Jeep lurched off the road and into a ditch.

"Out of the Jeep!" John yelled, pushing Jenny to exit the Jeep on the opposite side from where the shooting was coming. He followed her out; then both of them took cover in the ditch.

"Where the hell is he?" Jenny asked, looking up into the dark woods that climbed the hill on the other side of the road. "I can't see him!"

"Look for the muzzle flash," John said. "But be alert because the chances are he has a flash-suppressor. Most of the time the only ones who can see the muzzle flash are the ones who are being shot."

"That's a comforting thought," Jenny replied. John began stripping out of his shirt. "What are you going to do?"

"I'm going to give him a target," John answered. Feeling around in the ditch, he located a couple of broken branches. Sticking the branches into his shirt, then spreading them out so that the shirt was full, he held the shirt up above the lip of the ditch. "Keep your eyes open," he said.

They both saw it at the same time. A little wink of light, followed a second later by the sound of the shot. The bullet penetrated the shirt exactly where the heart would be. It was a frightening experience, but it did allow them to get a fix on Clay's location. He was 150 yards up the hill.

"Give him a target every now and then," John said. "But don't get too bold, he won't hesitate a second about shooting a woman."

"What do you mean, give him a target? What kind of a target?"

"Figure something out," John said. "What I need is for him to shoot often enough for me to be able to track him," John said. "I'm going after him."

"Yeah," Jenny replied. "You do that."

Staying low in the ditch, John crawled about fifty yards on up ahead of the Jeep. There, the road made a curve, and it was there that he darted across. He began climbing the hill then, moving slowly so as not to make any noise.

Cautiously, Jenny raised John's shirt again, exactly as he had done it earlier, by holding it spread open with the two branches. Clay shot again, and the impact of the bullet whipped the shirt from her hands. Retrieving the shirt, Jenny lay down in the bottom of the ditch, her chest heaving with fear and excitement.

John heard that shot, then a couple more, and knew that Jenny was doing her job of providing Clay with a target. He just hoped she wasn't giving him too much of a target.

Because of John's need for quiet, it took him almost fifteen minutes to traverse the distance between the Jeep and Sergeant Clay's firing position. Peering cautiously over a fallen and moss-covered tree trunk, John saw Sergeant Major Clay no more than fifteen feet away, leaning against a large, flat rock. Clay was staring intently toward the Jeep, on the road below.

The prime requirement for any sniper is absolute patience, and Sergeant Major Clay was certainly exhibiting that quality. Patience had never been one of John's strong suits, but then, he wasn't a sniper. Taking a deep breath, he raised up, leaped over the fallen tree, then rushed toward Clay.

It wasn't as foolhardy a move as it might seem. Clay was armed only with a rifle, and it was a long-barreled scoped weapon designed for long-distance killing. It was not a weapon that could be employed in close hand-to-hand combat, and John was closing the fifteen feet very rapidly.

Clay heard John coming toward him, and he raised up and turned, trying to swing his rifle around. But the weapon was too awkward and he was too slow. Before he could bring his weapon to bear, John sent the heel of his palm smashing into the base of Sergeant Major Clay's nose. The smashing blow broke Clay's nose, sending bone splinters into his brain. Clay was dead before he hit the ground.

Five minutes later, and with the spare tire on the Jeep, they were out on Highway 60, heading west toward Springfield at better than seventy miles per hour.

NINETEEN

Code Team Headquarters

John and Jenny, Paul and Linda, and Chris and Bob all arrived back in West Texas within a few hours of each other. Mike Rojas, who had drawn a complete blank in his investigation, had actually returned three days earlier. Shortly after everyone was back, they gathered in the conference room to compare notes. By now, Linda had told Paul about Ibo, and Paul made her share the story with everyone else. They had a good laugh when she described, in vivid detail, how she had convinced Ibo that she would meet him in the motel. They were still laughing when Don came into the room.

"I hate to interrupt the party," he said, "but I have just made an analysis of the situation, and I don't think you are going to like what I have discovered."

"What would that be?" John asked.

"The Oppressed Brotherhood is going to a meeting in St. Louis," Don said.

"Hell, I told you that," Paul said.

"That's right, you did," Don replied. "Freedom Nation is also going to a meeting in St. Louis."

"And I told you that," John said."

"All right," Don Yee replied with a smile. "But what neither one of you told me was, they're in cahoots."

"What?" John asked.

"Impossible," Paul added.

"I'll admit, it sounds far-fetched. But there is no way of getting around the facts. OB and FN are both going to St. Louis, not to bid against each other, but to make a joint purchase of the nuclear warhead," Don insisted.

"I don't get it. Why would two groups who hate each other as much as those two groups do form any kind of an alliance?" Paul asked.

"Perhaps to give them more strength against an enemy that is common to both of them," Jenny said.

"Who would that be?" Linda asked.

"The federal government?" Bob suggested.

"Wait a minute," Paul said. "John, Jenny, you may have something there. Damn, if I'm not beginning to buy into this. Freedom Nation wants to carve out a country for themselves up in the Northwest somewhere. And I wouldn't be surprised if Oppressed Brotherhood didn't have the same idea in mind. Not the same territory, but the same goal. Their own nation.

"Yeah," Paul went on. "About the only thing they agree on is how much they hate each other, and how much they want to segregate themselves from each other. I believe that, in their warped, evil minds, they have hit upon this as a way of handling that."

"Yes, well, it's good to talk about the theory," Don said. "But we have to look at something realistically, and that is, by joining their effort, the possibility that they will succeed in getting the nuclear weapon has just gone up exponentially."

"Don's right," John said. "We've got to get to St. Louis."

"I thought you might think that," Don said. "I've already arranged for a jet to meet you at San Angelo."

"How soon do we get started?" Bob Garrett asked.

John shook his head. "Sorry, Bob, but I think I'll keep this down to just the two teams who worked the two groups. We're already clued in on all the players. It'll be Paul and Linda, Jenny and me."

"Yeah," Bob said, obviously disappointed by the decision. "I was afraid you might call it that way."

"Don, get us an SUV laid on. Have it waiting for us at the airport in St. Louis. Paul, Linda, Jenny, what are you standing around here for?"

St. Louis

It took just over an hour and a half for the Learjet to reach St. Louis. Touching down at Lambert Field, the pilot taxied over to the General Aviation Terminal, where a Mid-Coast flight-line employee held up his batons to guide them to a parking spot. Looking through the window, Jenny noticed someone standing by the chain-link fence, holding up a sign with the name Paul Brewer. He was standing next to a Chevy Blazer.

"There's our wheels," Jenny said, nodding toward the SUV.

"Chevy Blazer," John said. "Wouldn't you think we deserved an Escalante, or a Navigator?"

"Yeah, or a Land Rover," Paul said.

"We're not going to a country club cotillion," Jenny said. "A Blazer is just fine."

At that moment one of the two pilots stepped back to open the door. "I hope you ladies enjoyed your flight," he said, smiling broadly at Jenny and Linda.

"What about us?" John quipped. "Don't you care if we enjoyed it?"

"Yes, of course," the pilot replied, flustered by John's remark.

Jenny laughed at John as they hurried toward the

Blazer. "What did you want to pick on our pilot for? I thought he was cute."

"You would," John grumbled.

"Mr. Brewer?" the young man with the sign asked as John, Jenny, Paul, and Linda approached him. All were carrying black, canvas bags.

"I'm Brewer," Paul said.

"Your keys, sir."

"Thanks," Paul said. He started to take out a bill, but the young man waved him off.

"No, sir, it's all taken care of, tip and everything," the attendant said. "And very generously, too, I might add. I don't know what company you work for, but they do know how to handle business."

"They do have a way of getting things done," Paul agreed.

As the four Code Name Team members were piling into the car, John's cell phone rang.

"Are you in St. Louis?" Don asked over the phone.

"Just got here," John replied. "We're pulling away from the airport now. Have you got any leads on where we should start?"

"More than a lead. I'd say this has a high degree of confidence. They're going to meet at the base of the north leg of the Arch at two P.M. You think you can be there by then?"

"That's twenty minutes from now," John said. "It'll be close, but I think we can do it." He punched off the call. "The Arch, and haul ass," John said as Paul pulled onto I-70.

"You got it," Paul replied.

Five minutes later, the scourge of all city drivers happened to them. Traffic in all lanes came to a complete halt as a result of a wreck half a mile up the road.

"Shit!" Jenny said. "Wouldn't you know it?"

"What now?" Paul asked.

"Will this help?" Linda asked, picking up a red rotating light.

"Where'd that come from?" John asked.

"It was under the seat. Don must've arranged for it to be put here."

"Wasn't he the smart one, though?" John said, putting the light on top of the car, then plugging it in to the DC outlet. The light began rotating a flashing red. "Okay, Paul, let's see what we can do with the shoulder."

Pulling off the road and onto the shoulder, Paul started up the highway, passing the seething drivers who were trapped in the congestion. When the Blazer got to the point of the wreck, they saw that the shoulder was blocked off by a couple of police cars. One of the patrolmen came back to talk to them.

"Can you get us through here?" John asked.

"Who are you?" he asked.

"Bomb disposal," John answered. "We've got a report of a bomb at the Arch. Listen, uh"—John read the policeman's name tag—"Patrolman Edwards. We really need you to get us through here."

"I'll do what I can," Edwards replied without asking for verification. Moving quickly, he got the two police cars pulled over to one side, then waved for Paul to be able to come through. It was a narrow passage, but once Paul was through, traffic became much lighter and he was able to drive at eighty miles an hour almost all the way to the Trans World Dome. He pulled into the Jefferson Memorial parking lot at one minute until two.

"All right, let's find 'em," John said as they got out of the car.

Jenny saw General Grant at almost the same moment Paul saw Kwazi. She and Paul spoke at the same time.

"There's Grant!"

"There's Kwazi!"

Grant and Kwazi were having a spirited with conversation with a rather smallish man who was clutching a canvas bag.

"I'll be damned," John said. "That's Carter Phillips."

"Who?" Linda asked.

"Carter Phillips," John said. "You know who he is, you've seen his picture on magazine covers."

"Yeah, I've heard of him," Paul said. "He's one of those dot-com billionaires, isn't he?"

"Not anymore," John said. "His company tanked."

"Looks like he's found himself another product," Jenny said.

"Jenny, you go to the right. Linda, you . . ."

That was as far as John got with his instructions. Grant and Kwazi saw them, and realized that if the four were together, something was going on. Both Kwazi and Grant were carrying canvas bags, and from those bags, they pulled out weapons, an Uzi for Kwazi and a MAC-10 for Grant.

John knew at once that if they opened fire, all the visitors to the Arch would be in danger. He started yelling at the visitors at the top of his voice. "Get down!" he shouted. He fired his own weapon into the air to frighten the tourists, and to get their attention. "Everyone, get down!"

Standing side by side, Kwazi and Grant, the two enemies, now formed an unholy alliance as they opened fire, spraying bullets all over. The visitors to the Arch screamed. The smart ones dropped to the ground, the unlucky ones began running. Many of those who ran were hit by stray bullets, and they went down as well.

Carter Phillips was shocked by the sudden and totally unexpected turn of events. "Have you two gone crazy?" he shouted. Like many of the tourists, Carter panicked and started to run. Grant turned his weapon on Carter and squeezed off a burst. Carter went down, and Grant grabbed the canvas bag.

"Let's go!" Grant shouted to Kwazi as the two men started toward the parking lot. But Kwazi was too fat and too slow to keep up with Grant.

"Wait for me!" Kwazi called.

Grant stopped, and for a moment it looked as if he would wait. Then, as if having second thoughts, he pointed his weapon at Kwazi.

"What? What are you doing?" Kwazi shouted.

"It would never have worked. You know that," Grant said. He pulled the trigger and Kwazi went down, spurting blood from his wounds. Grant jumped into his car, then peeled out of the parking lot.

Because of the crowd of tourists who had come to visit the Arch, John, Jenny, Paul, and Linda had been unable to return fire. Now, as they saw Grant speeding out of the parking lot, they hurried back to the Chevy Blazer. Grant had a head start on them, but they managed to catch up with him when he connected with I-55, heading south.

Without even taking aim, Grant held his MAC-10 out the window and, pointing behind him, began shooting. He didn't care who got in his line of fire. He knew there was little or no chance of hitting his pursuers, but that wasn't his purpose. His purpose was to create panic and confusion on the highway, and that was exactly what he did. Cars and trucks began weaving around wildly, trying to avoid the shooting. Many of them veered off, piling up in the median or on the shoulders of the highway, but the Chevy Blazer stuck doggedly to the chase.

By now, both the city and state police were involved, and several cop cars had joined the pursuit with lights and sirens going. The startled motorists who were heading north on I-55 were treated to the bizarre sight of a Buick being chased by a Chevy Blazer, being followed by twenty police cars, all doing nearly one hundred miles per hour.

South of St. Louis, Grant left the interestate and drove into the town of Bonne Terre. There, as he ran a red light, a pickup truck hit him broadside, causing the Buick to spin out of control. Paul pulled up behind him and the four Code Name Team members jumped out of the Blazer, all holding pistols pointed toward the Buick.

"Is he injured?" Jenny asked.

"I don't know. He took quite a hit," John replied.

"He's moving," Paul said, getting into position to watch him.

"Grant, get out!" John shouted at him. "Get out of the car!"

Slowly, Grant got out of the car. He was holding the MAC-10.

By now the police cars had pulled off the road as well, and dozens of policemen jumped out. They took up positions behind their cars, all of them pointing their weapons at Grant and the Code Name Team.

"Drop your guns!" a police lieutenant yelled at John and the others.

"Officer, we . . ." John started to reply.

"Drop them! Now!" the officer shouted.

"We'd better do as he says," Jenny said. Leaning over, she put her pistol on the ground. The other three followed suit.

"You, standing by the car!" the lieutenant shouted. "Put your gun down. Now!"

"You betrayed me, John. I thought, as warriors, we shared a bond. But like Judas, you betrayed me," Grant. He raised the gun to his temple.

"General Grant, no!" John shouted.

Grant pulled the trigger, fell back against the wrecked Buick, then tumbled forward, landing face-down. Dark crimson blood flowed from the wound in his temple.

John started toward him.

"Stay where you are!" the police lieutenant ordered.

"Officer, that man had a bomb," John said. "It may be armed." John noticed Patrolman Edwards among the group of policemen. Edwards was the officer who had helped them through the traffic connection. "Officer Edwards, tell them," John said.

"He may be telling the truth, Lieutenant," another policeman said. "I met them when they were on their way to the Arch. They're with bomb disposal."

"All right, take a look," the lieutenant said, waving toward the wrecked Buick with his revolver. "But if you make a move toward that weapon, we'll fire."

"Jenny, you want to come with me? I believe bombs are your bailiwick," John said.

Jenny looked toward the police lieutenant, and still holding his pistol on them, he nodded that she could go as well.

John and Jenny walked up to the car, then looked inside. The small canvas bag Grant had snatched from Carter Phillips was open. Inside the bag was a small, black device about the size of an older-model video camera. An LED readout read 0029:34. The 34 changed to 33, then to 32, clicking down one second at a time.

"Uh-oh," Jenny said.

"Uh-oh? What is uh-oh?"

"The son of a bitch armed the bomb. We have less than thirty minutes left before it goes off."

John turned toward the police lieutenant. "Lieutenant, you want to come over here and take a look at this?" he invited.

Cautiously, the lieutenant came up to the car. Then,

looking in through the window, he saw the bomb and the blinking timer.

"Damn," he said as he put his pistol away. "You were telling the truth."

"Yeah," John said grimly. Even as they were watching, the timer clicked from twenty-nine minutes down to twenty-eight minutes and fifty-nine seconds.

"Can you disarm it?" the lieutenant asked.

"What, you mean like cut the red wire but not the blue, the way they do it in the movies? No fucking way," Jenny answered.

Jenny's language surprised the police lieutenant, but he seemed more surprised that she couldn't disarm it. "I thought that's what bomb disposal people did," he said.

"I'm pretty sure it has a fail-safe device. If I attempt to disarm it, it will go off."

"You're pretty sure?" the lieutenant asked.

"With this bomb, pretty sure is enough," John said. "Lieutenant, you've got to evacuate the town now. There's no time to lose," John said.

"Are you kidding? There's now way we can evacuate this town in twenty-eight minutes," the lieutenant replied.

"We have to try."

"Why? I mean, how much damage can this thing do anyway? Looks to me like all we have to do is keep people away from the car for the next half hour. Then, after it goes off, it will all be over."

"It will all be over, all right," John said. "It will all be over for the whole town."

"What do you mean?"

"He means this isn't your run-of-the-mill blow-up-a-federal-building-type bomb," Jenny said. "This is a thermol-nuclear device."

"Thermol-nuclear device? I don't know what

that . . . holy shit! You mean this is a nuke?" The lieutenant's eyes went wide with shock and fear.

"That's exactly what I'm saying," Jenny said easily.

"My God! We've got to get out of here!"

"What about the town?" John asked.

"We'll drive through the streets using our PA system, but I don't know if . . ."

"Sir, if I could make a suggestion?" Patrolman Edwards said.

"What sort of suggestion?" the lieutenant asked, clearly agitated now by what he had stumbled into.

"A way we might be able to get out of this."

"By all means, Officer Edwards. If you have a suggestion, let's hear it," John said.

"Well, I'm from here, so I know this area pretty well. Nearly all these hills are dotted with old, deep, abandoned lead mines. Maybe we could get the people into those mines."

"I don't know. We can try, but I don't see how we can possibly . . ."

"Wait a minute!" Jenny said. "If the mountain won't come to Mohammed, Mohammed will go to the mountain."

"What the hell is that supposed to mean?" the lieutenant asked.

"You're talking about taking the bomb to one of those mines, aren't you?" John asked.

"Yes. The mine will not only buffer the blast and heat effect, but the lead residue should limit the radiation."

"How far to one of those mines?" John asked.

"The nearest one is about twenty miles from here."

"Twenty miles? We only have a little over twenty minutes remaining," Paul said. "We'll never make it."

"The hell we won't," John said, grabbing the bomb and running toward the Blazer. Jenny went with him.

"No, you stay back."

"If you run out of time, there's no way you can diffuse it," Jenny said. "I might be able to."

"I thought you said you couldn't."

"I probably can't . . . but if we are forced to try, I would have a better chance than you of doing it."

"I'll have to go, too," Edwards said. "Otherwise, you'll never find the mine."

"You sure you want to buy into this?" John asked.

Edwards nodded toward the town. "Like I said, I'm from Bonne Terre. I've still got family here. I wouldn't want to see my town blown away."

"All right. Come on."

John and the policeman hopped into the front seat. Jenny, with the bomb in her lap, crawled into the back. Paul and Linda started to get in as well, but John stopped them. He started the engine. "Look," he said through the open window. "The chances are very good that we aren't going to make it to the mine. And if that's so, there's no sense in all of us being vaporized."

"But we could . . ." Paul started to say.

His words were interrupted as John put the Blazer in drive. "Sorry, Paul, we don't have time to argue," he called back as he drove off, spraying gravel and spinning his tires on the pavement.

From the backseat, Jenny watched the LED for the timer, calling off the time remaining by the minute until she reached one minute. At one minute she started timing by seconds.

"How much farther is this damn mine?" John asked.

"There!" Edwards shouted, pointing up a small weed-filled gravel road toward a chain-link fence and gate. John whipped off the road and headed straight for the gate.

"Want me to get out and see if I can open it?" Patrolman Edwards asked.

"No time!" John replied, gunning the engine as he headed straight for the closed gate. Jenny was at forty-two seconds and counting when they crashed through the gate and drove up to the opening of the mine. The shaft opening was boarded over.

"We'll never get it deep enough into the shaft in time," Edwards said.

As they slid to a stop in front of the mine, John noticed a wooden chimney coming up from one side. "What's that?" he asked.

"An air vent," Edwards answered.

"How deep?"

Edwards smiled. "Deep," he said. "It goes all the way down, maybe a thousand to fifteen hundred feet."

"Thirty-one seconds!" Jenny called to them.

Taking the bomb from her, John tried to force it down the shaft, but it wouldn't go. "Damn!" he said. "I can't get it through."

He started trying to push the chimney over, but couldn't do it. Edwards started pushing with him, but even with both of them pushing, they couldn't get the chimney to go over.

"Get out of the way!" Jenny shouted, and they looked around just in time to jump to one side as she drove the Blazer up the side of the hill, straight at the wooden chimney shaft. She succeeded in knocking the wooden chimney over, but she also overturned the Blazer in the process. With the opening thus produced, John dropped the bomb down the shaft, noticing just as he released it that there were only nine seconds remaining on the timer. Looking over toward the overturned Blazer, he saw Jenny just getting up, stunned but unhurt.

"Get down!" he shouted as he and the patrolman ran to the overturned vehicle, dived over it, then got down on the other side. John pulled Jenny down with him.

There was a loud roar . . . followed by a column of smoke gushing up through the shaft. The earth trembled . . . but when it was over, it was over. Not so much as one tree was felled.

"You all right?" John asked.

"Yeah, I think so," Jenny said, feeling herself for any broken bones. "What about you?"

"I'm fine."

"Yeah, I am, too," Edwards said. "I may have pissed in my pants, but I'm not hurt."

"Let's get the Blazer upright, and get back to town," John suggested.

Because the Blazer was on its side and not on its back, and because it was rather precariously poised on the slope of the hill, righting it was not as much of a task as it could have been.

By the time they returned to town, the crowd had grown considerably. In addition to the state and local police, and the county sheriff and sheriff's deputies, the Feds had also been called out. FBI, CIA, and other federal officers were wandering around the scene, waiting to "congratulate" the people who had neutralized the bomb.

As they pulled up in the Blazer, John recognized several of the federal officers present. He realized at once that they weren't all here to congratulate them. They were here to, at worst, arrest them, and at best, ask several embarrassing questions.

"I think maybe we'd better get out of here," Paul said, coming over to the SUV.

"By now, every policeman in three states has a description of this Blazer," John said. "We'd better get another ride."

In the milling crowd, the four managed to sneak away. Linda found their ride, a state police car sitting at the rear end of the line. Looking in through the window, she saw that the patrolman had made it very convenient for anyone who would have the audacity to steal his car. Of course, he wasn't counting on people as audacious as the men and women of the Code Name Team.

"Damn . . . wish we could've hung around a little longer," Paul said as they headed toward St. Louis in the "borrowed" highway patrol cruiser.

"Why is that?" Linda asked.

"I read somewhere that Jesse James used to hide his gold in places like these old lead mines and caves. If there is anything buried down there, I'll just bet that bomb shook it loose."

"Yeah? What if he did, what good would it do you?" Jenny asked. "Anything in there will still be too hot to handle five thousand years from now."

"That's all right, I can wait," Paul said to the laughter of the others.

Don't miss William W. Johnstone's

next action/adventure novel,

ENEMY IN THE ASHES

Coming from Pinnacle Books in
September 2002!

(For a sneak preview of this novel,
just turn the page. . . .)

Claire Osterman drummed her fingers on her desk as her cold gaze roamed over the men sitting in her office. She'd called a meeting of her cabinet officers to discuss their current situation, and she wasn't happy with the news they'd been giving her.

Herb Knoff, her bodyguard and sometime lover, sat on her left, as usual. He was a large man with broad shoulders, coal-black hair, and a boyish face that belied his violent and unforgiving nature. The other men serving under Claire knew he was mean as a snake when riled, so they tried their best not to make him angry.

Claire glanced at Herb, a scornful expression on her face. "Herb," she asked in a low, dangerous voice, "can you believe this shit they're giving me?"

Herb smirked, shaking his head. "No, ma'am," he answered, his eyes narrow and flat.

Harlan Millard, Claire's official second in command in the government, a weak, mild-mannered man who was completely under Claire's thumb, held up his hand. "Now, Claire," he protested in his usual whining voice, "you asked us how things were. It's not our fault the situation is so bad."

Wallace W. Cox, Claire's Minister of Finance, cleared his throat and added, "That's right, Claire.

Things could be a lot worse. If Ben Raines and the troops from the SUSA hadn't intervened and helped us defeat those Middle Eastern terrorists, we could all be speaking Arabic now."

Claire fixed him with a steely glare. "How could things be worse, Wally? We may have won the war, but now you assholes sit here and tell me we're dead broke."

She stared at the other ministers in the room. "Hell, what good is it to win the war if we aren't left with enough money in the treasury to run the country?"

Clifford Ainsworth, Minister of Propaganda, nodded. "It's true that the treasury is at very low levels, Claire, but we weren't in all that good a shape even before the invasion by El Farrar's men. I'm afraid if we don't do something soon, the people are not going to stand for more restrictions in governmental services."

"Cliff's right," Gerald Boykin, Minister of Defense, agreed. "My troops haven't received a paycheck in over a month." He shook his head, a discouraged look on his face. "I don't know how much longer we'll be able to keep the soldiers in uniform if we don't come up with some way to pay them what we owe them."

Claire turned back to Cox. "I thought the United Nations had agreed to a loan package, Wally. Won't that bail us out until we can get the economy moving again?"

"It'll help some, Claire, but with half the country on welfare, the money they've promised us won't last six months."

"What the hell's wrong with everybody?" Claire asked, rolling her eyes. "Doesn't anyone want to work anymore?"

Ainsworth smirked. "Why should they, Claire, when

welfare pays them more for sitting home on their butts than they can make with a job?"

Claire stared hard at Ainsworth for a moment, and then she slammed her hand down on her desk. "Damnit, I'm tired of being told there's no money in the treasury and the government has to cut back while these layabouts are living off the government's tit. Cliff, I want you to announce immediately that due to the current emergency, all welfare checks will be cut by twenty percent."

Ainsworth's eyes opened wide. "But Claire, that'll cause riots in the streets."

She smiled grimly. "Good, then stopping them will give Boykin's troops something to do to earn their paychecks."

She got to her feet and leaned forward, her hands on her desk. "Now, get out of here and find me some way to get more money into our coffers. Raise taxes, or levy fines, or something. The government cannot function without money!"

Her cabinet members rose from their chairs, casting worried looks at one another as they filed out of her office.

Claire took a deep breath and stretched her arms out over her head. "Damn, these meetings always make me tense," she said, glancing at Herb Knoff, still sitting next to her. She gave him a half smile. "How about a massage for your boss?" she asked with a lascivious grin.

He returned the look. "Anytime is a good time for a full body rubdown, Claire."

She moved from behind the desk, took his hand, and led him into her living quarters adjacent to the office. As she went through the door, she began to unbutton her blouse.

Suddenly, a man dressed all in soldier's fatigues stepped from behind the door and whipped his left arm around Herb's forehead, stretching his head back while he put a long, curved knife to his neck.

"Holy shit!" Herb grunted, standing still as the razor-sharp blade drew a few drops of blood from his neck.

Claire whirled around, her hands going to her face. "What the hell's the meaning of this?" she almost shouted.

"My name is Muhammad Atwa," the man said in a heavy Middle Eastern accent. "I have a proposition for you, but I first need your assurance you will not summon help."

"How did you get in here?" Claire asked, her eyes flicking toward the phone on her bedside table.

Atwa moved the knife suggestively. "Please do not attempt to call for help," he said. "I am not afraid to die, and I most surely will kill you both before your guards arrive."

"I asked you how you got in here."

He shrugged, his lips curled in a cruel smirk. "Your soldiers are very lazy. Anyone in a uniform is allowed to pass almost without questions."

Claire sighed and sat on the edge of her bed. "What is it you want?"

Atwa reached around Herb's chest, took the pistol from the shoulder holster under his coat, and motioned for him to join Claire on the bed. Once Herb was sitting next to her, Atwa took a chair across the room and leaned back, crossing his legs with the pistol resting on his knee, the barrel pointed at them.

"I represent an organization based in Afghanistan."

"I thought we got rid of them back in the early part of the century," Claire said, her brow furrowed.

Atwa smiled again, though without the slightest bit of humor in his eyes. "Yes, that is what you thought. You did manage to kill our leader, Hajji Aziz, but we had others ready to take his place."

"And what proposition does Eternal Jihad have for the United States?" Claire asked.

"A friend of our organization, Abdullah El Farrar, has come to us with a plan to bring the world to its knees."

"El Farrar?" Herb asked. "Wasn't he the crazy bastard who led the terrorist attack against us this year?"

Atwa shrugged. "A misguided effort, as it turned out. He had neither the troops nor the materiel to complete his mission, though I think he would have succeeded had it not been for Ben Raines and the SUSA's intervention."

"I doubt it," Claire said. "We would have beaten him even without Raines and his troops. It would just have taken a little longer."

Atwa smiled again, showing he didn't believe her for a moment. "At any rate, the SUSA and the U.N. have frozen all of El Farrar's family's assets and he is very angry. He has come up with an intriguing scheme to make them pay for what they did to him."

"Yeah? And just what does he have in mind?" Claire asked.

"To take control of the world's oil supply," Atwa answered simply.

"Oh, is that all?" Herb asked scornfully.

"Let me explain," Atwa said, moving the pistol so it no longer pointed at them. "As you know, almost all of the working oil fields are in Saudi Arabia and Kuwait, since your country destroyed most of the others in Iran and Iraq during your little wars years ago."

"You're forgetting our fields in Alaska," Claire said.

Atwa waved a dismissive hand. "Yes, you have enormous reserves, but your environmentalists have so far blocked you from exploiting them to any degree."

Claire nodded grimly. The tree-huggers, as she called them, were the bane of her existence. She'd been trying for years to get the Congress to let her open up the fields to full production, but so far they'd resisted.

"So, how does El Farrar plan to take control of those oil fields?" Claire asked. "They are under the protection of the UN."

"My organization is prepared to put fifty thousand of our best troops at his disposal. He will use them to gain control of the oil fields and oust the U.N. troops, which are very poorly disciplined."

"So, and then what?" Claire asked. "Ben Raines and his SUSA troops would take them back in less time than it takes to tell it."

Atwa shook his head. "Not if you agree to help us."

"In what way could we help you?" Claire asked. "As much as I hate to admit it, our troops have never been a match for the SUSA's."

"We don't need your troops," Atwa said. "We merely need fifty pounds or so of the plutonium you have in storage."

"Plutonium?" Claire asked, puzzled. "You want to make an atom bomb?"

"No. We intend to place small amounts of the plutonium near all of the oil wells, rigged to explode if our demands are not met. As you know, plutonium is one of the dirtiest of all radioactive materials. If we set the bombs off, it will contaminate the oil reserves for thousands of years. The oil will be unusable."

"But," Claire said, horrified, "that would throw the world back into the Dark Ages."

"That is how we have been living in Afghanistan for decades," Atwa said, shrugging. "But I doubt it will come to that. Once the U.N. sees that we have the means and the will to destroy the world's oil supply, I think they will accede to our demands."

"And what will the United States get for our help?" Claire asked.

Atwa spread his hands, a wide-toothed grin on his

face. "Why, you'd get to be our partners in ruling the world, of course." He hesitated a moment, and then he added, "And Ben Raines would have to come crawling to you to get the oil his country needs to maintain their style of life."

The thought of Ben Raines having to beg her for anything decided Claire. She'd hated him for as long as she could remember, and now was her chance to get back at him for all he'd done to make her life miserable.

She stood up and stuck out her hand. "We'll do it!"

ABOUT THE AUTHOR

Bill Johnstone likes to hear from his readers. You can e-mail him at dogcia@aol.com.

THE *CODE NAME* SERIES
By William W. Johnstone

Today, when bomb-throwing madmen rule nations and crime cartels strangle the globe, justice demands extreme measures. For twenty years, ex-CIA agent John Barrone fought his country's dirty back-alley wars. Now, he spearheads a secret strike force of elite law enforcement and intelligence professionals on a seek-and-destroy mission against America's sworn enemies.

Be sure to order every book in this thrilling series from the master of adventure, **WILLIAM W. JOHNSTONE** . . .

___(#1) CODE NAME: PAYBACK
  0-7860-1085-1 $5.99US/$7.99CAN

___(#2) CODE NAME: SURVIVAL
  0-7860-1151-3 $5.99US/$7.99CAN
